MAGDA'S LADY

by the same author

novels
Natana
Kintalloch
The Hawthorn Hedge
Langwheeple
Wandering Angus

short stories
Teresa's Decision

translation
Weir de Hermiston i altres relats
(R. L. Stevenson's *Weir of Hermiston* in Catalan)

Magda's Lady

More Tales of Catalonia and Scotland

Mercedes Clarasó

BLACK ACE BOOKS

First published in 2007 by Black Ace Books
PO Box 7547, Perth, PH2 1AU, Scotland

www.blackacebooks.com

© Mercedes Clarasó 2007

Typeset in Scotland by Black Ace Editorial

Printed in England by CPI Antony Rowe
Bumper's Farm, Chippenham, Wiltshire, SN14 6LH

A CIP catalogue record for this book
is available from the British Library

ISBN 978–1872988-67–2

The publisher acknowledges support from the Scottish Arts Council towards the production of this volume.

Scottish
Arts Council

Aquest món, sia com sia,
tan divers, tan extens, tan temporal;
aquesta terra, amb tot lo que s'hi cria,
és ma pàtria . . .

This world, in all its forms,
so diverse, so wide, so temporal;
this earth, with all that finds life in it,
is my homeland . . .

Joan Maragall, '*Cant Espiritual*'

Contents

26

Magda's Lady

'But are they real, Irena? Are they really real?'

'Of course they're real, silly. I've seen them myself.'

'And they're alive? You're sure they're alive?'

'I've already told you. You can see them walking about. You've got to be alive to do that, you know.'

'I know, I know. But *how* can a living person be that big?'

'Well, they just are.'

More than anything else Magda wanted to see the *Gegants*, the giant figures that were to parade the streets of Barcelona on the feast day. Irena had told her they were as tall as the house, dressed in beautiful, flowing robes – and Irena should know, for she was eight years old. That was twice Magda's own age. And Irena had said the *Gegants* were more than twice the size of a grown man.

Much, much more than twice, Irena had added. And her little sister had gazed up at the older girl's earnest face, and been filled with wonder.

Twice something, she knew, meant it was very, very

big. And more than twice . . . It was almost beyond comprehension. And how could anyone, even a giant, be that big?

For days she thought of nothing else. Their parents had promised to take them to Barcelona that Sunday to see the *Gegants*. Irena was excited too, but not only about the *Gegants*. She had seen it all the previous year, and remembered the stalls, the noise, the crowds, the bands, the people dancing the sardana in front of the cathedral. She spoke of all this to her little sister, but nothing seemed to make an impression on Magda beyond the *Gegants*.

Among the endless questions she asked her sister and her parents there was one she always kept back – the really important one. Were the *Gegants* good? For suppose they weren't good – suppose they were wild and wicked, and chased you and hit you, and trampled you under their enormous feet?

Sometimes she was so overwhelmed by her fear of these monster figures that she wanted to ask her parents not to take her to Barcelona on that day. But she was afraid to admit her fear. And, besides, she was fascinated by these huge and wonderful beings. How could she renounce seeing them?

It was hot and dark and airless, standing in the crowd, with grown-ups packed closely all around her. All she could see was legs – some in skirts, some in trousers – and a number of handbags, one of which swung into her face.

'*Papa! papa!* I can't see. I can't see the *Gegants*!'

'They're not here yet. I'll pick you up as soon as they appear,' her father reassured her.

They were standing in one of the narrow streets in the

Gothic quarter of the city, near the ancient Church of the Pine Tree. The crowds were pressed against the tall buildings to leave a space in the centre for the expected procession.

'*Ara! Ara vénen!*'

As the cry rang through the crowd Magda's father bent down and put his arms round her.

'Here they come,' he said. 'Up with you!'

Magda felt herself being raised, floating up, into a world of joy and excitement, tinged with a slight frisson of fear. For what if they were wicked after all, these huge and wonderful creatures?

Further along, she could see a giant figure advancing slowly and majestically. Behind it she made out another, and then yet another.

'Three!' she exclaimed.

Irena had told her there were only two. In her mind she settled it that this third giant was there specially for her, her own *Gegant*. Of course, if they weren't good after all, these enormous beings, perhaps she didn't really want one of her own.

As the first figure came near enough for her to make out the features her fear disappeared immediately. She had never seen anything so beautiful, so calm and stately as the face that was approaching, gazing impassively ahead. The figure was dressed in long, flowing robes of a soft, purple material.

Longer than curtains, thought Magda, as she watched the skirts almost sweeping the ground. Then she lifted her gaze again to the figure's head, and realized that a golden crown sat on the dark hair.

A queen!

Magda's awe was boundless.

Slow as was the advance of the giant figures, the first one passed too soon for the delighted Magda. But a moment later the second one had come up. Instead of a crown this one wore a silver diadem studded with jewels. The dress was of a shiny material in bright greens and yellows. The effect was dazzling. This figure too had a calm and beautiful face, and moved past with the same graceful, flowing movement of her long skirts.

And now my one, thought Magda, straining to see every detail of the final figure.

And this one, oh, this was the loveliest of them all! The long, rich folds of her silky skirt were of a soft, dove grey; her bodice was a warm, glowing pink; in one hand she carried a lace fan; and her face was even more beautiful than the other two, for there was a soft, almost tender expression on the perfect features.

Magda was enraptured. This was the best, the loveliest of the three, and she was *her* lady. For she no longer thought of them as giants, but as ladies, one of them no less than a queen.

Like the previous figures, this one turned occasionally towards the watching crowd on either side, with a slight inclination. And little Magda, perched high on her father's shoulder, received one of these acknowledgements.

From that moment she knew she belonged to her lady, fully, freely, for ever.

As soon as the figure had passed, her father put Magda down, with the words:

'You're getting to be quite a weight now, Magda.'

The child was filled with desolation. So that was it! Her idol had passed, she wouldn't see her again.

She was about to burst into tears when a daring idea came to her. At that moment neither parent held her by the hand. She was free! Without a second's hesitation she darted into the crowd and began making her way through it, in the direction of the departed *Gegants*.

It didn't take her long to catch up with the soft grey cloud of her idol's skirt. She ran right up to it, picked it up by the hem, and slipped inside.

At first she could hardly see, in the dim, grey light of the moving tent. She was surrounded by soft folds of grey, flowing gently along. I'm in a cloud, she thought, I'm in a cloud and the cloud is my lady, and I'm part of it too.

She was floating along, hearing the crowd all round her, but not part of it. She was part of the soft grey cloud which was her lady. The thought made her feel immensely privileged.

After she had got used to the half-light she looked about her to see the feet of her idol, and was puzzled to see only two long poles moving forward, one after another. Looking up she could make out nothing, as the darkness increased higher up.

For a moment she was disconcerted. Where, then, were her lady's feet?

A voice in the crowd started singing, and this distracted her. Other voices joined in, and soon the whole crowd was singing:

> *Els gegants de Pi*
> *ara passen, ara passen.*
> *Els gegants del Pi*
> *ara passen pel camí.*

Magda recognized the old song, which generations of children had sung before her. Taking courage from her sheltered solitude, she joined in:

> *Els gegants de la Ciutat*
> *ara ballen, ara ballen.*
> *Els gegants de la ciutat*
> *ara ballen pel terrat.*

The song had always conjured up a vague vision of the *Gegants* from the Church of the Pine Tree walking through the streets, while the *Gegants* from the City danced on the roof. Now she knew what it was all about. The *Gegants del Pi* were, at this very moment, walking through the streets, and she was walking with them, she was one of them – or, at least, she decided, thinking of her own small form, she was one of their chosen followers.

Gradually the singing began to die out, and another sound replaced it. Voices were calling out:

'Magda! Nena! *On és la Magda?*'

More and more voices were calling her name, and they were the voices of strangers. Further back in the crowd she could hear a woman crying hysterically.

And still the torrent of strange voices, all calling her name:

'Magda! Magda!'

She was filled with terror. What did all these strangers want of her? What were they going to do to her?

Would her lady not help her, protect her? In her fear she clasped one of the poles that were walking along beside her. There was a sudden jerk, and then, as the two poles staggered about drunkenly for a moment, a man's voice a long way above her, letting out a stream of guttural oaths.

'My lady!' she cried, terrified. 'My lady!' She grabbed an armful of the soft grey material, trying to wrap herself up in the cloud.

Just then unknown hands unwrapped her, and a strange man picked her up and held her high in the air.

'*Es aquí! Es aquí la nena!*'

A moment later, just as she had begun to scream in terror, her father appeared and took her in his arms. Behind him came her mother, with tears streaming down her face.

People were shouting, laughing, enjoying the joke.

Fancy hiding under the skirts of one of the *Gegants*! What an idea!

'I'd give her a good hiding, that'll teach her not to run away from her parents.'

Magda, in spite of her relief at being rescued from the crowd and handed over to her parents, was crying bitterly.

'My lady!' she sobbed, 'My lady!' That a being so gracious, so wonderful and magical, could turn into two long poles and a handful of grey cloth?

They didn't know what she was talking about, and she was never able to explain her heartbreak.

27

The Sweet and Pungent Air

Alistair lay back on the rough ground and thought: now I'm really here, on Catalan soil. Those few days in Barcelona with Rachel didn't count. Could have been anywhere, any big city on the face of the earth. But now I'm in touch with the earth. I can pick up a handful of the very soil – dry, gritty, a mixture of sand and gravel with just a little red almost-powdery stuff thrown in, a whole lot of tiny seeds, fragments of dried roots and one small, bewildered ant, hurrying from my wrist to my fingers and back again.

There you go, little ant, I don't want to keep you from your business. I know you've a lot to do.

He'd really enjoyed the walk in the sun after getting out of the car, with its stormy atmosphere. The first mile on foot had been wonderful – sun, a hard-baked track under his feet leading upwards and upwards into these delightful little hills smelling of rosemary and other herbs he couldn't identify. What a cocktail! he thought, breathing in the heady aroma.

In the end the heat had become a little too much for

him, and he had made for the nearest tree.

Perhaps he should have waited till the sun was a little lower before getting out of the car. But such practical considerations had been far from his mind when he made the move.

Without warning, Alistair had stopped the car.

Rachel looked at him enquiringly.

'Why are we stopping?'

'I'm getting out.'

'What for?'

'For good.'

As he spoke he leaned over to the back seat and grabbed his rucksack and his jacket.

'But . . . '

'You go on,' he said. 'It's your car, after all.'

'But how are you going to get back to Barcelona?'

'I'm not going back.'

'But the hotel . . . the room—'

'You can have it to yourself. Or share it with one of those handsome young Spaniards. As you please. I couldn't care less.'

He got out of the car and started walking along the little track on his left. After a moment he heard the engine starting up and the car driving off. He didn't look back.

Well, what was I expecting? he had asked himself. Did I really think she would get out and plead with me? Did I want her to? Doesn't matter, anyway, now. I'll probably never see her again. Does that matter? Yes, it does, for it means I'm free.

After a few more minutes of trudging through the

afternoon heat he came to the conclusion that the parting was definitely for the best. It had been a glorious, blazing, intoxicating affair, but nothing more. And it had spent itself. This holiday had shown him just how little they had in common. Rachel had been blissfully happy in Barcelona – the bars, the restaurants, the nightclubs. This, for her, was what a famous city was all about. And for the first few days Alistair had agreed with her. But all the time he was looking forward to seeing the Catalonia his father had so often talked about.

As a student in the 1960s – just as the first waves of tourists were beginning to 'discover', and so transform, Spain's coastline – Alistair senior had visited the ancient monastery of Santes Creus. After the rush and noise and glare of the seaside resorts, he had been enchanted by the stillness, the solidity, the mere age of this Cistercian monastery, and was anxious for his son to have the same enlarging experience. And Alistair had been more than willing to promise.

But it turned out that even half a day was more than Rachel would willingly devote to looking at 'a heap of old stones buried in the countryside'.

In the end she had agreed, grudgingly, and they set off about midday, both of them in a rather edgy mood, aware that a disagreement was looming. And it might have been all right if they hadn't lost their way. But after nearly an hour of wandering about looking for encouraging signposts, Rachel had made it clear that the only sensible thing to do was go back to Barcelona and forget all about 'this stupid medieval business'.

With each uncertain mile the emotional temperature had risen till it reached boiling point.

And now he was free. Free to go to Santes Creus or anywhere else he felt like. He'd got his rucksack, his documents, money. No transport, but that might perhaps be an advantage for the sort of holiday he now had in mind. And he was enjoying the walk. All the more so because he didn't know where he was and where this track might lead. But it's bound to lead somewhere, he thought, and somewhere, anywhere, will do.

For a moment his equanimity was ruffled by the suspicion that perhaps he shouldn't have left Rachel alone in a foreign land. Would she be all right? He answered his doubts with a ringing *Yes*. Rachel was, after all, a perfect example of the twenty-first-century young woman – confident, capable, determined. She'd be all right.

As for him, he was going to enjoy this holiday in his own way. He would see Santes Creus, yes, but that need not be today. By stepping out of the car he had eradicated time. He could take as long as he liked about finding the place. And meanwhile, he was here.

And here was strange and new and full of surprises. He would at some point, no doubt, meet one of the natives. Till then he would just saunter along, taking in the details of this new landscape. Everything dry and dusty, the track rising higher into the hills all the time . . . It was all just as his father had described.

After a while the heat had prompted him to leave the track and make for a nearby group of trees. He sat down in the shade of the nearest and looked up at it, wondering what kind it was, with its tall, straight, slender trunk, its branches spreading out symmetrically, its long light green leaves hanging absolutely still.

He lay on his back, enjoying the pattern of the leaves

against the vivid blue sky, and thought of how often he had lain like this on Scottish soil, looking at rather different leaves – rowan, beech, or birch – outlined against a less blue sky. It was a familiar situation, yet here everything was different, strange, new – and yet, uncannily familiar.

It was good to be here, away from the city's cosmopolitan bustle, here, on Catalan soil.

Quite literally, he thought as he wriggled about on his stony bed. In his new position he had a slightly different view of the branches above, and noticed a little group of something more solid than leaves. Fruit of some kind, he assumed, and stood up to examine the phenomenon more carefully.

The branch was just beyond his reach. With a little jump he managed to get hold of one of the objects and pull it off the branch.

'*Ep, tu, què fas?*'

With a start he turned round. A man was freewheeling down the track on a small motorbike. He now stopped and glared at Alistair, signalling him to come closer.

Feeling like a little boy caught stealing apples, Alistair complied, holding the object of his theft in his hand. He had no idea what this small, green, furry thing could be, and would have liked an explanation from the stranger, who, in his turn, seemed more intent on getting an explanation than giving one.

The man, still astride the bike, was haranguing him in a language Alistair could make nothing of. Catalan, he presumed, for it didn't sound at all like the few phrases of Spanish he had learned. He made out a reference to the Civil Guard, after which the man indicated that the intruder was to get on the bike behind him.

It was not a prepossessing invitation. Alistair hesitated, reviewing his options. Given that the language barrier prevented him from offering any excuse or explanation he decided he'd better comply, in the hope that the Civil Guard would surely provide something in the way of an interpreter.

In silence he mounted behind his captor, and the bike roared into action. Soon they had joined the road where he had stepped out of the car, and in a few more minutes they reached a village and drew up in front of what looked like the town hall, with two Civil Guards standing at the door. No English spoken here either, but Alistair understood someone was being sent for, and in a minute a middle-aged man, appeared, went up to Alistair and held out his hand, saying:

'Francesc Berenguer, at your service.'

'Oh, you speak English?'

'I spent five years in London in my youth, just to learn the language properly. I gather that Bofill here is accusing you of theft. What precisely have you taken from him?'

Alistair put his hand in his pocket and produced the small furry object.

'This. But I don't actually know what it is.'

Francesc laughed.

'I see, you have been robbing him of his almond crop. A serious accusation,' he said with mock solemnity.

'So it's an almond! I'd never have guessed. I didn't know they looked like that on the tree.'

Bofill bounced forward and took the almond from Alistair, while the two Civil Guards looked on phlegmatically.

After a brief conversation with Bofill, Francesc turned to Alistair.

'I've given him my word that I'll see to it you do no more pilfering, so you'd better come with me. I know it seems an awful fuss to make about one almond, but the people from the city do sometimes cause a lot of damage, tearing branches off, and helping themselves to large quantities of anything they can get – grapes, for instance, in the vineyards. Come, this way.'

They had only gone a few steps when Bofill caught up with them.

'*Té,*' he said, holding out the almond of contention.

Alistair took it and thanked him.

'Tell him I'll treasure this,' he said to Francesc.

They were walking along a wide, straight street made up of terraced houses with huge wooden doors, most of them open to reveal a tiled vestibule with a glass inner door. There were plane trees at intervals along the street, but apart from that no sign of vegetation. And, at that time of the afternoon, with the sun beating down, not a human being in sight.

Inside Francesc's house it was so cool that Alistair felt as if he'd stepped into a cold shower.

'Let's go through to the *eixida*,' said his host. 'It only gets the sun in the morning, so we'll be cool there.'

They went along a tiled hall which widened into a spacious dining room, and then through glass doors into a patio surrounded by extremely high walls covered with exotic-looking creepers. There were several fruit trees, large bushes in brilliant bloom, and a number of big ceramic pots with flowers spilling out of them. At the far end of the patio there was something like a huge, tiled basin with an ornamental fish leaning out of the wall above it, pouring a jet of sparkling water into the tank.

Alistair gazed at it in admiration. Some water feature! he thought.

'That's the *safareig*,' explained Francesc. 'For washing clothes. Long ago, that is. All the old houses had their *safareig* and some of us keep them just for their beauty, and the soothing sound of running water.'

'This is a fantastic place. And what a contrast! Everything so hot and dry outside, and here it's cool and shady and sheltered and . . . and moist.'

'But you have this contrast too, in your country. Only the water and the cold are outside, and the heat inside. We all need contrast, we live by opposites.'

Francesc went into the house to get some drinks, and Alistair wandered about the *eixida*, taking in the variety of plants, shrubs, bushes and trees. Most of them he found he couldn't even put a name to. Geraniums, yes, he thought, I recognize them. And those great glowing globes up in that tree are oranges. As for the rest, it's all new, stunningly new.

'You know,' he said some time later as they sat in the shade sipping their chilled white wine, 'all this, it's wonderful, fantastic, like something out of *The Arabian Nights' Entertainments*. And yet . . . well, remember I spoke about the contrast between this and the hot, dry, almost arid outside?'

Francesc nodded. 'I think I know what you're going to tell me,' he said. 'You're going to say you actually prefer the hot dry version, is that it?'

'How did you know?'

'You gave me a verbal clue. "And yet . . . " Besides which, it's the way I feel too. That's why I live here.'

Alistair looked at him, puzzled.

Francesc stood up. 'Come and see.'

He led the way to the back of the patio, where, almost hidden by the branches of a huge climbing vine, was a small wooden door. He opened the door, and Alistair took a step back, almost dazzled by the blaze of light that met them. Through the doorway he saw a gentle slope of exactly the same type of low scrub that had so impressed him an hour or two earlier. The heavy perfume of the lilies in the patio was replaced by the light, spicy aroma of herbs.

Alistair stepped through and, without thinking about it, squatted down and started running his hands lightly through the different tufts at his feet. 'The smell!' he said. 'The wonderful, pungent smell! What are they all? These incredible little shrubs?'

'They're nature's first gift to medicine. Pretty useful in the kitchen too. Stay for a meal and you'll see.'

After the meal Francesc and his wife Teresina prevailed on him to stay the night as well.

'Is good to have again a young person,' she explained in her broken English. Their children had all grown up and left home. 'They no like the village.'

'No, I'm afraid we're too rustic for them,' added Francesc. 'They couldn't wait to get away.'

'And I'm the opposite. I'd like to stay here for ever,' sighed Alistair.

'Then why don't you?'

'Because it's just not feasible. How could I earn my living here when I don't even speak the language?'

'You speak the most useful language in the world. There's a huge demand for English-teaching here.'

'I know. That's what my father wanted to do when he fell in love with this country. But he had his career to think of, and he was engaged to my mother. And she would never have agreed. So, you see, he was committed.'

'And are you?'

Alistair looked at Francesc, startled. 'N–no . . . not to a person. But there's my career.'

'Doing what?'

'Oh, computers. Like everyone else.'

'You don't sound very enthusiastic.'

'It's all right. Quite a good way to make money.'

'You still don't sound enthusiastic,' Francesc repeated.

'Is good,' came from Teresina, with a nod of approval.

'What's good?'

Teresina found it hard to explain in English, and her husband had to interpret for her.

'She thinks it's good that you're not too enthusiastic about a job that seems to have nothing but a good salary to recommend it. And I think so too.'

Alistair smiled.

'I see I'm outnumbered,' was his only comment, and the subject was dropped.

But when they left him alone in the big, old-fashioned bedroom upstairs he spent a long time at the window, looking at the faint outline of the hills just beyond the village and thinking the unthinkable idea his hosts had put into his head. Could he really give up the life that had been mapped out for him, just to follow this newly discovered longing for a fragrant hillside?

For hours the argument raged in him. There were all sorts of common-sense reasons for ignoring the madcap suggestion. But there were reasons in favour as well. After all, he was young, he had all his life before him, and he would never be freer than he was now. Even the tenuous thread that bound him to Rachel had been broken. He tried to imagine how she would have reacted to the idea of his giving everything up to come over here and settle down to life as an obscure English teacher. He nearly burst out laughing at the thought.

Eventually he fell asleep. In the morning he woke very early, feeling refreshed and eager to explore this new world. The sun was just rising, and a great silence hung over the village. He tiptoed downstairs and let himself into the patio. The whole place was dim and shadowy, even more mysterious than it had appeared in full daylight. He made for the little door and opened it.

There, he thought, that's it, the world I'm looking for.

He found a large granite stone and sat down on it. The level rays of the sun still lacked enough heat to draw out the various smells of the different herbs, and he neither saw nor heard any insects. He sensed a great, waiting stillness all around.

As the sun rose higher, he became aware of tiny movements near his feet. First an ant appeared – much larger than the one he had seen yesterday. It was followed by another, and another, then more and more. A solid column of ants was moving from the roots of a fennel plant, heading for a clump of thyme. He recognized these two herbs, for Francesc had taught him their names the previous afternoon. A few small birds – some kind of finch, perhaps – fluttered out of a nearby almond tree, which he now recognized from the previous day.

He reflected that twenty-four hours earlier he wouldn't have been able to identify any of this vegetation. I'm learning, he thought with a little thrill. But he just couldn't make out why it seemed so important for him to observe and understand everything in this new world. Heredity? he wondered. Wasn't this the world his father had fallen in love with?

After a while he got up and started walking about the hillside, taking care not to lose sight of Francesc's back door. Never before had he been so aware of the ground under his feet, of his connection with the earth. It was as if he himself was a part of his surroundings. As if he had spent his life in exile, and had at last come home. He simply couldn't explain it, and wondered if there was any need to try. What's the point of trying to explain a gut feeling? he thought.

So he decided that was the matter settled. He had made his decision. He turned back towards the house and found Francesc standing in the frame of the little door.

'I thought that's where I'd find you. Come and have breakfast.'

Teresina met him with a smile. 'Ah, you have not escapated. Is good.'

'Not yet. But I'm leaving today.' Alistair enjoyed the sudden consternation on Teresina's face.

'You go back to Barcelona?'

'No, to London, and then back to Scotland.'

Francesc seemed just as surprised and disappointed. 'But why, Alistair? As we say here, what fly has bitten you?'

'I've made my decision, and I'm going back right

away. To tell my parents and to hand in my resignation.'

'And after that?'

Husband and wife spoke together, still anxious.

'After that, will you take me in as a paying guest till I find something of my own?'

After a celebratory breakfast, Alistair crossed the patio and went through the little door for a last few minutes on the hillside. The sun was now high enough to release all the scents from the varied herbs and bushes. As he left, he turned at the door to the patio and breathed in one last lungful of the sweet and pungent air.

'I'll be back!' he pledged aloud.

28

Deil's Leap

'Lemme go! Lemme go!'

The child was screaming, struggling to get free.

A moment later her cry had changed to 'Dinnie let go! Dinnie let go!' as the big man lifted her up and swung her out over the low parapet, dangling her above the precipice.

He was laughing.

'Weel, whit is't ye want? Am ah tae let go or no?'

By now the child was too terrified to do anything but scream, as the man swung her from side to side over the abyss.

'Sae ye want tae flee, Lintie? Lintie wants tae flee! Up ye go, Lintie, high, high up! Fleein, fleein! Wee Lintie's fleein!'

At last he put the little girl down on the ground. She ran off, sobbing hysterically all the way to the village a hundred yards down the road.

Jamie continued his walk, slightly puzzled by her reaction. She had said she wanted to fly, after all.

Jamie and Lintie had gone up the hill road together,

as they often did. They were buddies, and had been ever since the tiny Lintie was old enough to wander the village streets on her own. Lintie's endless curiosity about the natural world had delighted Jamie, who had been happy to share with her the secrets of where the siskins were nesting, how to approach old Mrs Baird's bad-tempered dog without being snapped at, how you could tell where the fox had been prowling, and how the russet-coloured beech hedge managed to turn green all over in a matter of hours.

'Look! See a' they wee pointed spears? They're the new leaves, rolled up like an umbrella, waitin for a nice warm day tae uncurl. They're rust-coloured on the ootside, which is the back o' the leaf, and that's a' ye can see till they open up. And they're bricht, bricht green inside. Sae, whan they a' open up, the hale hedge turns green.'

Lintie, who had been astonished at the sudden change from rust to fresh young green, was enchanted at this explanation. It confirmed her belief that Jamie was the cleverest man in the village; for she'd asked several other people for an explanation, and had got nothing but indifference. Nobody knew and nobody cared.

Jamie, at twenty-two, had perhaps the intelligence of a normal seven-year-old, so he was the perfect companion for the endlessly inquiring little girl. He was good-natured and harmless, though not always perfectly sensible. He was accepted in the village, for he was always willing to use his great strength for the benefit of anyone who needed a hand with shovelling snow, carrying bricks or clearing out an old shed. But his concentration was so poor that he could never be left to get on with a job on his own, so fixed employment was out of the question. And his limited understanding meant that he had no friends of his own age. Only a few of the children would let him join in their games. He would have been a lonely figure, had it not been for the intrepid Lintie, who shared none of the fears which his bulk and his reputation as feeble-minded inspired in the others.

On the surface Jamie was accepted; but deep down many of the villagers felt some repugnance towards this huge, dim-witted creature whom they sensed as something alien and unpredictable.

They were buddies, Jamie and Lintie, but they had their ups and downs, for both of them enjoyed what they thought of as a good joke. This meant that Lintie sometimes teased Jamie, and Jamie sometimes teased Lintie. As a result they had the odd quarrel, which was usually made up by the offer of some new-found treasure – a spray of hawthorn from Jamie, with the thorns carefully removed, or half a Mars bar from Lintie.

On this occasion the two friends were sauntering up the hill road, and Lintie had been admiring the flight of a seagull, as it dived and rose and swooped above the great gulf of the Deil's Leap, where the land dropped away sharply from the side of the road.

'Oh, ah wish ah could flee! Ah wish ah could flee!' Lintie had exclaimed passionately.

'Aye, ah ken. Ah've aye wantit tae flee.' And all the longing Jamie had always felt to be rid of his great, heavy body, and to fly and float and soar and swoop through the air, gliding effortlessly and at random, like a wisp of thistledown; all this longing was suddenly transformed, as he realized he could get his little friend to do the flying for him.

Without warning he pounced on Lintie, seizing both her arms in his great fists. And Lintie had screamed and struggled to get free.

Lintie's mother, at first, did not believe her story of being held over the precipice. She knew Lintie to be an intense little creature, given to exaggeration. Certainly, she was very distressed at the moment; but surely Jamie wouldn't be daft enough to swing her out over Deil's Leap? And then she noticed the bruising on the two frail arms where the strong hands had held her.

'Martha!' she called to her neighbour. 'Come and see this!'

'Whit is it, Nell?'

The two women agreed that this time Lintie must be telling the unvarnished truth.

'Jist wait till ah get him!'

'Jist wait till ah get him an a',' chimed Martha.

Martha's four-year-old had come in crying with fright several times because 'the daft man' had spoken to her in the street. And he had recently played one of his pranks on her twelve-year-old, who had been foolish enough to believe Jamie when he said he'd seen a peregrine falcon up the hill, only to be laughed at heartily when he came back disappointed. For some time Martha had felt someone ought to teach Jamie a lesson. His latest exploit was just what she wanted. She set about spreading the news of Jamie's latest offence.

'Terrified the bairn oot o' her wits . . . Near killt the lassie . . . Whit if he'd droppit her . . . ? Jist aboot dislocatit her puir wee arms . . . Covered in bruises, puir wee mite!'

* * *

Half an hour later Jamie was on his way back down to the village. He had seen many things he would have enjoyed sharing with Lintie. She would have loved seeing the first bright flowers of the broom, the long, trailing white clouds to the west, the great stone he had found with tiny sparkling bits all through it. She would have asked what it was and he'd have said it was silver, even though he had a suspicion it couldn't possibly be anything so precious. It was a big stone, too big to carry. He'd tried to chip a bit of it off by hitting it with another large stone, and it had broken in two. So he'd picked up one of the pieces and, heavy as it was, he was carrying it back for Lintie. This was to be the peace offering.

As he turned into the village street he was confronted by a row of women standing shoulder to shoulder. Lintie's mother stood in front of them all.

'Pit that muckle rock doon,' she commanded. 'Ye've done enough mischief for ane day.'

'Mischief? Me? Ah havnae done a thing!'

'Ye tried to kill ma wee Lintie.'

At first Jamie couldn't understand what she meant. 'Ah niver! Me kill Lintie? Ye must be mad.'

'Ye swung her oot owre the Deil's Leap.'

'Oh, that! Ah was helpin her tae flee. She said she wantit—'

'Never mind whit she said. She cam hame covered in bruises and frichtened to death. And ah've already telt ye tae pit that rock doon.'

'Ah'm no pittin it doon. It's for Lintie.'

At this point the men began coming in from the fields.

'Whit's gaun on here?

A babble of voices answered:

'He tried tae kill Lintie.'

'He jist aboot threw her owre the Deil's Leap.'

'He wants tae kill her wi this great rock he's carryin.'

All the suspicion, all the imagined grievances, all their fear of the abnormal, came rushing out. Boys who'd had a disagreement with Jamie over the rules of a game, mothers whose children had been knocked over by him on the football pitch, neighbours who complained that he woke them up in the morning with his raucous singing . . .

For Jamie sang. Loudly and joyfully, he would express his satisfaction with the world in song. His powerful baritone would burst forth, fortissimo, at any moment of the day or night. And first thing in the morning, long before his hard-working neighbours were ready to face the day's toil, thunderous snatches of anything from *Nessun Dorma* to the latest pop tunes would ring out.

'But ah'm happy,' he would say to protesters. 'Ah sing because ah'm happy. Sing wi me! Be happy wi me!'

But today nobody wanted to sing with Jamie. They didn't want his kind of happiness.

And now a strange new elation had seized them. They felt united as never before. They had come together in defence of an innocent child, and so felt justified in giving vent to all their resentment, irritation and hidden fears. The spirit of the mob had taken over.

The men, each assuming the role of vigilante, pushed their way forward, past the women.

Andy Pearson stood out in front of them all. Andy had old scores to settle with Jamie, for Jamie was the only one who could beat him at any of the trials of strength the men sometimes indulged in. Andy could toss the caber further than any other man in the village – except Jamie. He could control an angry bull better than any man – except Jamie. He could lift more bales of straw than any man – except Jamie.

Andy Pearson was more eager to have a go at Jamie than any man in the village.

'Get back up the hill,' he said. 'We dinnae want ye here. Ye're a danger tae the community.'

'But ah've no done oniething!'

'Ye tried tae kill Lintie!'

'Ye nearly threw her owre the Deil's Leap!'

'If she hadnae managed to struggle free . . . '

The flood of accusations drowned his protestations for a moment. Then he proclaimed:

'She wantit tae flee. Ah was just helpin her. Ah've aye wantit tae flee an' a'.'

'Get back up that road and right oot the village, or we'll help ye dae a bit o fleeing a' richt,' was Andy's retort.

This sally brought forth cries of approval:

'That's richt!'

'A taste o' his ane medicine!'

'Back up tae the Deil's Leap wi' him!'

Andy took a step forward.

'Gie's that rock!' he commanded.

Jamie shook his head.

Andy took another step forward, which brought him within inches of his adversary, and held out his hands for the stone.

Jamie took a step backwards. 'You're no gettin it.'

Again Andy advanced, followed by the crowd, and

Jamie retreated, still clutching his rock.

The crowd was urging Andy on. Again and again he moved one pace forward, and Jamie retreated, one step at a time, up towards where the road overlooked the Deil's Leap.

As the tension increased, as they drew nearer to the precipice, the voices died down. Slowly, and in utter silence, the procession moved on up the hill. One step at a time, the crowd was forcing Jamie back to the precipice.

Nell had put Lintie to bed and sat with her till the child fell asleep, tired out with her fright. Then Nell went out and joined Martha in stirring up public feeling against the insane idiot who was terrorizing their children, as it now appeared.

Lintie woke up feeling refreshed, and perhaps just a little ashamed of the fuss she had made. She was, after all, a big girl now – seven years old! As on many a previous occasion, she knew she could actually have stopped crying earlier. Great as her fright had been while 'flying' above the precipice, by the time she reached the village she was no longer in any danger, and could have controlled her outcry. But her fear had been superseded by anger, and she wanted Jamie punished for what he had done. So she had kept up the crying.

She got up and started going downstairs, not quite sure what line to adopt. Would she complain again of her bruises, to justify her panic and tears, or would she just go and tackle Jamie herself? It would really depend on how her mother was taking the affair.

But the house was empty. She stepped out into the

street, and the street was empty too. Puzzled, she walked along, past Martha's house, past old Mrs Baird's house with the dog tied up by the door, giving the animal a wide berth, just in case. But this time it paid no attention to her, for it was straining at its leash, doing its best to follow the crowd up the hill road. Lintie walked on, past a few more houses, till she came to the cottage where old Mrs Muir sat in her wheelchair.

As soon as she saw Lintie, the old woman cried out:

'Mercy, child, are ye a' richt?'

Lintie wished she hadn't been crying quite so loud or quite so long, as she had passed the cottage on her way home.

'Course ah'm a' richt. Whar's a'body?'

'They're a' up the hill road, chasin Jamie.'

'Whit for? Whit's he done?'

'Done? He tried to kill ye, did he no?'

Lintie didn't wait.

Jamie and his pursuers had got to Deil's Leap.

He stood with his back to the drop, facing his aggressors. Andy was standing a couple of paces away. He was the first to break the long silence:

'Sae ye want tae flee, div ye?'

Jamie said nothing.

'Ye ken,' remarked Andy, 'accidents can happen. Ye micht jist happen tae fa'owre the edge, here. That's whit a'body would think, if ye was fun deed at the bottom. Especially ainse they kent you was keen on fleein. They would a' say, "Puir Jamie! Thocht he could flee owre the Deil's Leap! Puir Jamie! But then, he wasnae a' that bricht, was he? No quite a hunner per cent."'

'Is that why ye want tae kill me? Because ah'm no a hunner per cent? Because ye think ah'm daft?'

'No. Because ye tried tae kill Lintie.'

'Ah didnae, ah tell ye. Ah didnae! And if ye dinnae believe me, ask Lintie. She'll tell ye hersel'. Ah wud never hairm her. No Lintie.'

Nell spoke up:

'But ye did an a', Jamie. Whit aboot a' they bruises on her puir wee arms?'

'Ah didnae mean tae hurt her. Ah never thocht. She kens fine ah never meant tae hurt her. Jist ask her. Let's go and get her.'

'She's owre ill. Lyin in her bed, quite feverish she wis, whan ah left her.'

Andy Pearson, beginning to feel the role of principal was slipping away from him, said:

'Ye neednae think ye're gaun tae get her or onie-yin else. Ye'll jist stey there, wi' yer back to the Deil's Leap, till we've decidit whit tae dae wi' ye. Ye're a public menace, and we've got tae protect oor bairns frae the likes o' you.' Andy took another step forward, so that he was now only a few inches from his adversary.

Jamie gave a quick glance behind him, saw just how near he was to the low parapet, and tried to edge nearer the middle of the road. But the villagers quickly stepped in to fill the gap. Jamie had no space in front of him, and all the space in the world behind him.

For the first time he realized the gravity of the situation, and a great fear showed in his eyes. Still clutching his stone, he called upon the only power who could save him.

'Lintie!' he cried out, '*Lintie!* Come quick!' His huge

voice echoed down the hill.

And from below came Lintie's shrill little voice:

'Ah'm comin, Jamie. Ah'm comin.'

All the villagers turned round and saw Lintie's small figure running up the hill towards them. She arrived, panting, and they made way for her.

'Jamie! Jamie! Whit's wrang?'

'Look, Lintie, ah've brocht ye a stane. A rare muckle stane, wi' sparkly bits!'

Jamie knelt down and put the stone on the ground in front of Lintie. She knelt too, and began tracing the shiny bits with her forefinger, forgetful of her grudge.

'Oh Jamie, it's lovely. Is it siller?'

'Looks like it. But ah dinnae really ken, like.'

'Come on, let's tak it hame.'

Lintie stood up and signalled to Jamie to pick up the stone. He obeyed, and the pair set off. The crowd, which had closed in round them, opened up to let them through. Then, rather sheepishly, the villagers all followed the two friends, who were chatting away merrily, their differences forgotten along with their fears.

Gradually the men and women began talking too, eager to forget their recent ferocity as well as their sudden volte-face.

'That taucht him a lesson, oniehow.'

'Needed a bit o' a scare, he did.'

'Aye, he really thocht we wis gaun tae push him owre.'

'As if we'd iver hae dune sic a like thing!'

'Course no!'

'There's nae harm in the laddie, really.'

Andy, scowling furiously, pushed his way through the crowd and hurried past the two reunited friends, muttering something about having better things to do than play with children.

And the crowd, seeing him stride off, found their new scapegoat, and murmured that they thought he really did mean to push poor Jamie over the cliff edge.

'Puir Jamie! He means weel enow.'

'No like that yin.'

'Oh, that yin!' with a look at the receding Andy.

'Yon's a thrawn bugger, yon!'

'Ah've aye thocht there was something no canny aboot him.'

'Richt eneuch, see last week?. . . '

By the time they all got home their world order had been restored.

29

Disasters teach us

The woman was labouring up the steep path that led from the village to her employer's house. She was carrying a large basket with parcels of meat and fish, two bottles of mineral water and one bottle of wine. She also had two string bags full of fruit and vegetables.

She was such a slight figure, so tiny, that it seemed as if her burden must weigh more than she did. But, slowly and steadily, frail but determined, she made her way up the path. Everything about her person was grey – her clothes, her hair, her skin, and her eyes – beautiful, gleaming eyes, that sometimes sparkled with a hint of ironical amusement. They looked surprisingly young, set in that wrinkled, weather-beaten face.

'*Bon dia, Marcela.*'

'*Buenos días tenga usted,*' she replied with the courtesy and gravity typical of the Andalusian servant of her time, ignoring the fact that she had been addressed in Catalan, a language that she, as an outsider, refused to speak. She stepped aside to leave room for the neighbour who was overtaking her on the narrow path.

The younger woman paused for a minute. She looked as if she was going to say something, then changed her mind and went on ahead.

Marcela watched her for a moment before resuming her climb.

Yes, yes, you're dying to ask me all about it. But you've a bit of a problem, haven't you? It's your pride that keeps you, a señora, from indulging in a private conversation with a servant! And yet, you suspect I could tell you the very thing you're dying to know.

She picked up the basket she had set down, and started toiling up the hill again.

As if I'd have told you, anyway! I've learned the value of silence in my long life, believe me! I learned it that day thirty years ago, when I overheard my first mistress scolding her daughter.

'But Mamá, Marcela says—'

'You don't listen to what Marcela says. She's only a servant.'

That was my lesson. A hard one, learned the very first week I was in service. Not so many months earlier I had been the mistress, with a servant of my own. Did I treat her like that? I wondered then. And I'm still wondering. It takes a lot to make us see things from the other's point of view. Something big, really big. A civil war, for instance.

When she got to the house she was still thinking about the Civil War, how they had knocked on the door one night and taken Antonio and shot him. It was just after they had done the same with García Lorca. Just the same, except that Antonio wasn't a famous poet, so nobody ever knew about it except for his family and friends. And there were so many killed in the same way, God rest their souls, she thought, and crossed herself as she made her way through from the kitchen to tell doña Remedios she was back.

Doña Remedios was in the bedroom, trying to decide whether to get dressed.

'For I'm certainly not going out today, Marcela, you understand. I am indisposed.'

'Yes, señora, that's what I said to all the people who were asking after you.'

'All the people? Were there many?'

'The señora has many friends.'

'I see.' Doña Remedios knew how to interpret her servant's tactful generalizations. 'Do you think, Marcela, do you think they . . . heard anything?'

Marcela, remembering the series of frantic screams and furious roars that had issued from the sitting room when don Pedro had come home just before midnight, could think of nothing more reassuring by way of an answer than a tiny, unobtrusive shrug, while her face remained impassive, with downcast eyes.

Doña Remedios sighed.

'I wish . . . I wish I could go out as usual and meet them all with my customary composure. That would stop their tongues wagging, all right. But, of course . . . ' Doña Remedios sighed again. ' . . . that's out of the question.'

'Yes, señora, out of the question for a few days,' replied Marcela, discreetly refraining from looking at her mistress' two black eyes.

'And tell me, did they ask about my indisposition? What did you say?'

'I told them that the señora was suffering from a common feminine complaint.'

Her mistress nodded, without noticing the ironic gleam in her servant's eyes, provoked by the reflection, that this complaint was indeed only too common among the female population. Adultery, along with its consequences, was the most exciting thing these women ever came across.

But why do they want all this excitement? she wondered. Well, I suppose we wanted it too, long ago, before we knew the price one has to pay. We got excitement all right when the war came and turned everybody's life upside down.

Her own life, certainly, because the war had taken her husband, and he was all she had. No children, no near relations of her own, and no friends who could afford to be seen helping the widow of a supposed Red.

A few days after the assassination she decided she would run the business in his place. It was the least she could do for Antonio's memory. He had inherited a carrier's business from his father, just a couple of mules and a few ancient carts, carrying goods to and from all the villages round about. Furniture, building materials, livestock, a new pulley for old Francisco's well, an icebox for the village inn . . .

But the son had bigger ideas, and he worked, and he introduced first one lorry, and then another, and another, till his was the biggest firm for many villages around, and employed quite a few men. And he had always discussed the business with Marcela, so she knew she'd be able to keep it going, for they had good men working for them.

It would be a relief too, being so immersed in the work; it would dull some of the pain of Antonio's loss.

After the first few days she realized that they were getting no new orders, and soon she came to see that the business had virtually melted away. In the atmosphere of fear and mistrust that the war had brought nobody wished to be seen supporting the firm of an alleged Red. Was the fact that he had been shot by the Civil Guard not proof enough that this was where his sympathies lay?

When the bank account was empty she sold her furniture and used the money to pay her fare to the opposite corner of Spain, for she couldn't bear the shame of going into service locally.

Thirty years later, as she was preparing the midday meal in another woman's house, and wondering what to do about the present tricky situation, her mistress appeared, worried.

'Did you tell the *peinadora* not to come?'

'Yes, señora, I passed by the hairdresser's and told the girl you were too unwell to have your hair put up.'

'You think of everything, Marcela.'

'It's my job, señora.' But Marcela reflected that it took a crisis like the present to have her worth acknowledged in this way.

Doña Remedios sighed. 'I look so terrible like this, with my hair down, and . . . '

Marcela came to her rescue. 'It's beautiful hair, señora, and in a few days all will be well. The sun will shine – it always does – the birds will sing, the honeysuckle will smell better than ever, and all will have been forgotten.'

'Oh, Marcela, I wish I could be as confident as you! What makes you so optimistic?'

'Disasters, señora. Disasters.'

Doña Remedios gave Marcela a wavering look. She didn't always know how to take this servant of hers.

Later on one of the neighbours called at the kitchen door:

'Is doña Remedios all right, Marcela?'

'She has one of her little indispositions. Why are you asking?'

'Because of all the uproar last night, just after don Pedro came home. It was earlier than anyone expected, so we wondered—'

'Uproar? What uproar?'

'Didn't you hear it? Screams and shouting, such a noise!'

Marcela fixed her grey eyes on the neighbour.

'I heard no uproar. I heard nothing. Must have been those gypsies again, going back to their camp.'

Cowed, the neighbour retreated.

Virgen Santísima! Why do I have to tell so many lies? thought Marcela. Is it simply to keep my job? But she knew it wasn't that. Thirty years of impeccable service had given Marcela a reputation she could count on.

Wondering where her loyalties should lie in the present situation, she went over the facts once again, in a dispassionate attempt at clarity.

The facts were these:

The previous night don Pedro had come home earlier than expected, only to discover doña Remedios in intimate converse with the young chemist, Miguel Prados. Marcela did not know quite what degree of intimacy the conversation had achieved. Suffice it to say that don Pedro had thought it justified his throwing the young man out bodily, and then giving his wife a good beating.

It certainly looked suspicious. As the whole village knew, Don Pedro had been summoned to a family discussion in Barcelona that afternoon, and was not expected home till very late at night – at least two or three in the morning. It seemed rather a strange coincidence that the chemist should turn up, uninvited, after dark, on precisely that evening. Marcela strongly suspected that the wife had informed the dashing Miguel Prados of this happy opportunity for a tête-à-tête. That very morning there had indeed been a note for the chemist. In itself this was not unusual, for doña Remedios sometimes got him to make up a special lotion for her delicate skin.

In spite of her suspicions, Marcela was very upset on hearing her mistress's cries for help. In the end, alarmed, she had dared to enter the *sala* unbidden and intervened on the terrified wife's behalf. Don Pedro coped with this interruption by threatening Marcela with dismissal, and his wife with expulsion; after which he strode off indignantly, leaving Marcela to comfort the afflicted wife and bathe her eyes in rose water.

Up till this point the relationship between the two women had been strictly that of mistress and servant. They got on well together, but each remained within her own sphere. They spoke amicably of the work to be done each day, of the price of fish, of the latest tittle-tattle, of the new schoolteacher and the fear that if it didn't rain soon they would have to bring in water restrictions. But nothing private, nothing personal, except on the most superficial level.

'Have you seen the new house the judge is having built, Marcela? Beautiful, isn't it?'

Marcela, who thought the new building hideous and

ostentatious, would raise a deprecating hand, incline her head almost as if in a tentative bow, and say:

'*Mire usted*, señora. We all have our tastes, have we not? And I, personally, perhaps because I'm just a plain woman, I prefer something simpler.'

And her mistress would agree that tastes differ, and they would agree to disagree in perfect amity. But they never went any deeper than that in the matter of personal preferences or feelings.

And now, as Marcela ministered to her afflicted mistress, she realized that this very act was establishing a bond between them. Here she was, playing the part of nurse, friend, mother even, to this woman who was, and must remain, her mistress.

And Marcela was also aware of another ambiguity. For now that a quarrel had erupted between husband and wife, she had placed herself clearly on the woman's side; and yet don Pedro was her employer, her master, *el señor*. Besides which, not only did she like the man, in spite of his somewhat violent temper, but she strongly suspected that his indignation was fully justified, if perhaps expressed in rather too forcible a manner.

And so, the morning after the explosion, Marcela had been careful to treat her mistress with her usual calm deference. Her master had not appeared all morning, which was causing Marcela some concern. Never before had he failed to turn up for breakfast. Late in the morning he had left the house, without speaking to either of the women.

While Marcela was still puzzling over the situation, doña Remedios came to the kitchen again. By now she was dressed, but with less care than usual. She was a pretty woman in her early thirties, with long golden hair and an almost childlike softness of feature. With her hair hanging loose and her bruised face she looked appealing, pathetic even. I must defend her, thought Marcela, even though I'm almost sure she's been betraying her husband with that young jackanapes of a Miguel Prados – and with others too, most likely. But she's a child, a wayward child, and don Pedro is far too solemn and severe for her. And so, right or wrong – and I suspect it's probably wrong – I was right to take her side and defend her.

'You spoke about disasters, Marcela. You said that disasters make you optimistic. I just don't understand.'

Marcela looked at the tearful face of her mistress, and fought off the impulse to take her in her arms and comfort her.

'The señora is very young. It's difficult to understand these things till you're old, like me. Then you learn that life is full of paradox.'

'Paradox? What does that mean?'

Marcela regretted having used a word that she, as a servant, could hardly be expected to know, and which was evidently unknown to her mistress.

'It means that things are sometimes the opposite of what they seem.'

'Oh, Marcela, that's too complicated for me. I just want to be happy, and to enjoy myself.'

'Of course, señora, that's what we all want. Only, there are different ways. And disasters teach us.'

'To get what we want?'

'To want what we get, señora. And that is a far more valuable lesson.'

Just then they heard don Pedro coming into the house.

'Remedios! Marcela! I want you here, in the *sala*.'

Doña Remedios turned pale.

'Oh, Marcela, I'm so afraid!'

'It will be all right, señora.'

But Marcela too felt apprehensive as she followed her mistress along the corridor and into the drawing room.

Don Pedro was standing against the window, presenting a tall, massive and imposing outline. It was impossible to make out his expression as he stood against the light; but every line of his body spoke of affront and determination.

'I have been making inquiries,' he stated, 'and I have found out that you, Marcela, paid a visit to the chemist's shop yesterday morning, and handed a note to the chemist. You refused to give it to the assistant, alleging that it was for don Miguel himself. It presumably contained the valuable information that I was to be out all evening, and well into the night. Now, you, Remedios, assured me last night that you were not expecting this visit, and that, flustered as you were by finding yourself *unexpectedly* alone with this man (and he stressed the adverb with great emphasis), you allowed yourself to be carried beyond the normal limits of decorum.'

Pompous ass, thought Marcela, and then realized what he was getting at. Of course, she thought, he's looking for a way out, a way of forgiving his wife without losing his dignity.

'So,' continued don Pedro, 'if that is the case, the real culprit is the go-between, the organizer, perhaps even instigator, of the whole pathetic business. Marcela, do you deny that you took a note to the chemist?'

'I could not deny it, even if I wished to. There were witnesses.'

'Exactly! And what, may I ask, was in that note?'

Marcela turned to her mistress.

'Señora—'

Doña Remedios raised her bruised face and looked her husband straight in the eyes.

'I sent no note,' she said, with a firmness of voice that astonished Marcela.

Betrayed! thought the servant. She has betrayed me! And immediately her resentment turned to pity, as she realized the weakness that had prompted this betrayal. The injured husband had thrown the wife a lifeline, and she was only too thankful to seize it.

'And how much did he pay you for this piece of valuable information?'

'Nothing, señor.'

'How much?' he boomed.

Marcela stood silent, knowing the only possible outcome of the interview. Don Pedro was too anxious to be convinced of his wife's near innocence to listen to any protestations she, Marcela, might make. All she would achieve would be to destroy the wife's precarious safety.

One hour later she left the house, with all her belongings tied up in two bundles. Without hesitating she made for the station. No point in looking for another place in the village, having left this one under such a cloud.

As she sat on a bench on the platform waiting for the next train, Marcela murmured:

'Disasters, disasters! I suppose it was about time for the next one, after so long. It wouldn't do to lose the habit, would it?'

She stood up, for the train was approaching. As she waited for the passengers to alight, one of them recognized and greeted her, gazing in astonishment at the two bundles.

Marcela smiled politely and bowed with her usual dignity.

'*Buenos días tenga usted,*' she said.

Then she picked up her bundles and stepped lightly up into the carriage.

30

Briefest Encounter

I knew I'd find him waiting for me further along the road. I was looking forward to the meeting with this stranger; but I didn't hurry. I hadn't had my fill of the little hollow that had seduced me as I drove along.

It was the green, the radiant, glowing green, of the grass on either side of the mountain stream that had called me. Set in the rich, warm colour of the peaty hillside, this hollow radiated light and energy, with the sparkling water dancing along its bed.

I had parked the car on the only few yards of level ground at the side of the narrow, twisting road. And when another car appeared, going in the same direction, the driver and I waved to each other, as people do when they meet in wild, solitary places like this one on the imposing shoulder of Schiehallion.

The driver slowed down, looking for some place to park. But I had taken the only available space. That was when I knew I'd find him waiting for me.

Every time I came here I felt my emotional temperature drop as I left this special mountain and headed for the Lowlands. This time I suspected there might be some consolation waiting for me along the road.

The car was parked just before the first junction. As I approached, the driver got out and started walking towards me. I drew in and lowered my window.

For a long time we talked – about Schiehallion, the mighty giant, and the spell it always cast on both of us.

'It's the Mons Grampius of the Romans,' he remarked.

Of all the things we said, that is the one sentence that has remained with me over the years. Perhaps because it encapsulated all the awe and respect with which the mountain has been viewed throughout the ages.

As I drove on, downhill, downhill all the way, I felt I had a stronger, more enduring link with the beloved mountain. My feet were on sea level, but my spirits refused to be dragged down. All these years later I still remember the green, green patch of grass with the sparkling burn running through it. I still remember how I once shared my passion for Schiehallion with a stranger on the mountainside.

31

Venturet and the Pig

Venturet knew the exact moment his grandfather died. The old man had become very quiet, and hardly seemed to be breathing. Venturet was kneeling on the floor beside the ancient mattress. In his ten years the boy had seen a few deaths on this same palliasse – his mother and father last year, dying within a few days of each other when the typhoid fever had swept through the village; his big brother before that, as a result of that fall from the scaffolding in front of the church.

Venturet was watching carefully, determined that this time he would actually catch sight of the spirit as it left the body. He was fond of his grandfather, who had been both mother and father to him since the death of his parents, and knew he would miss him, for he would now be left alone; but he was sustained by the knowledge that this time he would be sure to see the spirit as it escaped its earthly bonds and floated up to heaven.

He hoped it wouldn't be much longer now, for he was getting very hungry, and he knew there was some bread in the kitchen, and half an onion. But he simply daren't take his eyes off the old man, in case he missed the moment of death. He knew his grandfather would not deliberately deprive him of witnessing the great event, but he also knew that the exact time of death was not in the hands of the sufferer. So he knelt there, tired, stiff and hungry, waiting patiently.

And at last his patience was rewarded. The old man made a sound that was not quite a sigh, not quite a cough, and Venturet saw something white and wispy detach itself from the recumbent form and float away towards the door.

Enthralled, Venturet stood up, ready to follow it outside the hut and watch it winging its way to heaven.

Just as the departing soul was reaching the door, their neighbour's pig appeared on the threshold, raised its head in a practised gesture, and swallowed the migrating object. The pig was used to catching its food on the wing as Curro's wife threw scraps of food to it out of the window.

Venturet was appalled at this unheard-of disaster. He knew, from the conversation of the villagers, that all sorts of hazards had to be faced by the soul on its way to heaven, purgatory or hell. Evil spirits lay in wait for it; wolves had been known to come down from the mountains and tear it to pieces; the Devil himself was not above seizing it and carrying it off to undeserved damnation. But to fall victim to a neighbour's pig!

The boy was deeply concerned on his grandfather's account. He was also disappointed that he had not been able to witness the flight of the soul as it made its way to the heavenly gates, to see what St Peter had to say to it.

This latter disappointment was mitigated by the long-awaited bread and onion, and by the reflection that at least this time he had actually seen the soul as it left the body of the departed – a white, filmy substance, just as he had been led to expect. That was surely the most important thing. Now he knew beyond the shadow of a doubt that the soul does actually exist and that it is a visible object. Nothing could persuade him that he had imagined this departing soul, or that it had been nothing more than the play of a beam of light through the open window. He knew, positively and conclusively *knew*, that the soul existed, and that it floated out of the body at the moment of death.

And he also knew that this particular soul had been devoured by Curro's pig. This knowledge posed some rather serious problems. For one thing, the pig in question, like most of his brethren in the community, was due to be slaughtered in a few days' time, at the Feast of St John. And what, he would like to know, would happen to his grandfather's soul after that? Would it be able to escape and wing its way up to St Peter? And would St Peter not be angry at the delay? Would he really believe this story about being swallowed by a pig? In all the wealth of folk tale and superstition with which Venturet had been brought up, there had been no hint of a similar misfortune befalling any soul, alive or dead.

As he ate his bread and onion he kept his eyes on the pig, which had trotted back to Curro's corral, where it belonged. So far Venturet's relations with the animal had been of the friendliest, for it was a sociable creature, and was always happy to let him scratch it between the ears. They had even taken a walk together on several occasions, and Venturet had gone the length of christening it Pepote, a name that seemed to him to suggest the round-bellied, friendly, easy-going nature of the beast The boy had been viewing its approaching sacrifice with more than a little sadness. His present feelings, he had to admit, had changed somewhat. He couldn't help suspecting that the pig had behaved badly in the matter of the old man's soul. It had presented Venturet with a problem he simply didn't know how to solve. How could he possibly allow the animal to be slaughtered, when it was the container, the host, one might say, of his grandfather's soul? On the other hand, how could he prevent this sacrilegious slaughter?

Both Curro and his wife Martina had always shown affection for Venturet. Martina had even gone as far as saying that, once *l'avi* was dead – he had been ill for some time, and they all knew he was dying – she and Curro would do what they could for the boy. But Venturet was too much of a realist to feel there was any possibility of their sparing the pig, even for the sake of their old neighbour's soul. Anyway, they simply wouldn't believe him. Who ever heard of a pig swallowing the soul of a grandfather, no matter whose?

After a while he decided he would have to leave the problem of the soul unsolved for the time being, for he knew what had to be done in the event of a death. He must tell Martina, who would come and lay out the corpse; he must see the priest to make the funeral arrangements; and then he must go round all the houses in the village to make sure everyone knew about the death. A funeral was a matter of great concern to all, and not one of them would think of missing the ceremony.

As chief mourner, Venturet followed the coffin to the church the next day, and sat, and stood, and knelt through the service with all the customary devotion and sorrow. That, at least, was the impression he gave. But his grief was tempered by the increasing urgency of coming to some conclusion as to what was to be done to prevent the slaughter of the pig that housed his grandfather's soul.

For what would happen to that soul when Pepote fell victim to the butcher's knife? Would the soul die a second time? This, surely, would be most unfair. And would a soul proceeding from the body of a pig be acceptable to the Most High? He suspected that nobody, not even the priest himself, would have a conclusive answer to those questions. And, unless he could have an absolute guarantee that his *avi's* soul would not be in any way imperilled by the pig's demise, it was clearly his duty to make sure that the pig was not slain.

His metaphysical questioning was interrupted by a sudden inspiration. Sanctuary, of course! Therein lay salvation. All he had to do was get the pig into the church, and no-one would dare lay a finger on it. Wasn't that what churches were for? He had heard many tales of robbers and bandits who had sought, and found, sanctuary within the walls of the church. And as long as they remained inside those four holy walls, no-one, not even the king, could touch them, however many gruesome murders they might have committed. And this was only a relatively innocent animal!

Along with Venturet's conviction of what to do came the knowledge of how to set about it. He must wait till it was dark, then bring the pig along to the church and stay with it till the priest came the following morning.

He would then explain the problem, and the priest would undoubtedly agree to this stratagem to save the soul of one of his parishioners. Father Isidre was a good man, deeply devoted to the salvation of souls. He would certainly agree that the pig must be saved, even if it meant accepting a strange new member of his flock.

That night Venturet waited till long after all the lights had gone out in the village before creeping into Curro's corral and gently tying a piece of rope round Pepote's neck. Then he stood up and tugged at the rope. A few contented grunts were all the response Pepote vouchsafed. He seemed to consider the process as some sort of endearment, the equivalent of the already familiar and much appreciated head-scratching.

In the end Venturet had to sacrifice a portion of the bread he had stuffed in his pocket, to be eaten at leisure in the church once his mission was accomplished. By holding the bread within sniffing distance of Pepote's snout he succeeded in awakening the animal's interest. A hasty withdrawal of the proffered snack achieved the desired result, and Pepote struggled to his feet and advanced on the tempting morsel.

Venturet took care to keep the bread well out of the animal's reach, and so they stumbled through the village till they came to the church. As expected, the church was unlocked. Pushing hard against the massive door, the boy opened it and advanced, bread in hand, and Pepote followed. For a moment, once he had got the door shut, Venturet was tempted to eat the bread himself, but reflected that this would be a bit unfair on the pig. Even though he was doing it to save the animal's life, you could hardly expect the creature to appreciate this. So he handed over the promised reward, and settled down to eating his own share.

The church had always inspired him with awe and admiration, being by far the biggest building he had ever seen. Now he found that it was more impressive than hospitable, and wandered about for some time, looking for a comfortable place to sleep. Everything seemed very cold and hard and unwelcoming. Perhaps inside one of the confessionals? But that, he suspected, might be sacrilege. He felt he was treading on rather thin ice as it was. No need to complicate matters further. He settled for a corner near the door, and curled up on the floor, where Pepote soon joined him. He was glad of the animal's warmth, and the feeling of not being quite alone in this big, empty, holy place.

He was awakened by a yell of indignation.

'*Demonios!*' had exclaimed Father Isidre, on catching sight of a pig in his church.

'Don't let it out, Father, don't let it out!'

Venturet rushed forward, past the pig, past the priest, and banged the door shut.

Father Isidre turned a look of mingled surprise and indignation on his young parishioner. He was a corpulent, large-bellied man, perhaps a little too fond of the good things of this life for one of his calling, but generally well disposed. A bit like Pepote, it struck Venturet for the first time.

With unwonted severity the priest now asked Venturet what he was doing in the church at this time of the morning, in the company of a pig.

'We've been here all night,' replied the boy.

'That explains nothing. *Why* are you here, both of you? That is the question.'

'Please, Father, we've come for sanctuary.'

The priest looked from Venturet to Pepote.

'I can see why that one might be seeking sanctuary, with the Feast of St John only two days away. But I don't see that *you're* likely to be in any danger. They wouldn't get many rashers out of *you*, would they?'

Venturet was relieved at the jocular manner in which the priest was taking the matter. At least he wasn't angry, that was something. But would it be easy to persuade him of the seriousness and urgency of the matter?

'The problem is', he announced, 'that I'm very worried about my grandfather's soul.'

'But your grandfather was a good, God-fearing man. His soul, I'd stake my life on it, is right now doing a short stint in purgatory, from which he will soon be released to fly up to heaven with the blessed angels.'

Venturet shook his head lugubriously.

'His soul, if you'll forgive me, Father, is right inside that pig.'

The priest listened in silence while Venturet explained his dilemma. Then he stood looking at the boy with a puzzled expression. At last he moved forward, laid a hand on Venturet's shoulder, and said:

'I think I know the answer, Venturet. But you must promise me never, but never, to breathe a word of it to a living soul, for this is a very delicate matter, and not everyone would understand. So do you promise, most solemnly promise, that you will keep total silence about the whole affair?'

'Yes, Father. I promise.'

'Right, then. Have you ever heard of exorcism?'

'Yes, Father. It's something to do with casting out devils, isn't it?'

'Yes . . . that's the usual form.' Father Isidre seemed a little taken aback. Then, recovering his aplomb, he continued. 'But there's also a special version for . . . for occasions similar to this.'

'You mean this has happened before?' Venturet suddenly had a vision of all the pigs in Christendom keeping a lookout for any departing souls to be snapped up. But if this was a common danger, why had no-one ever mentioned it before?

'Not exactly in this form. But there is a formula of exorcism for the restitution of any soul that has been, as it were, misappropriated by some other being, as in this case. And we'd better do it right away, before Ramoneta comes to clean the church.'

Father Isidre stood in front of the pig and began muttering unintelligible words, much the same as during mass. At the same time he made the sign of the cross repeatedly:

'*Anima praeclari avi Ludovici, ego te impero ex corpore porculi exire et ad coelestes regiones ascendere. In nomine Patris*, etc . . . . Amen.'

'Amen,' said Venturet with fervour.

There was a moment's silence, and then the priest said in his ordinary voice:

'Well, that's it. Your grandfather's soul has been released, and is right now on its way to St Peter, who will, of course, know all about what happened by now. He's always kept informed in cases of exorcism. So that's the matter settled.'

'But . . . but I didn't see the soul coming out of the pig!'

'I'm not surprised. It was in such a hurry, it simply flashed past,' said Father Isidre, as he bent down to pat the pig on the head. 'I hardly saw it myself.'

32

Danger Zone

There was no reason why that particular bit of road should make him feel uncomfortable. Exactly the same as the preceding stretch. Straight, level, with the asphalt merging into grass at both sides. Clumps of gorse here and there. An open sweep of grass to the left, rising gently to a bare horizon about half a mile away. To the right, the ground sloping almost imperceptibly down to the cliffs, with the sea beneath them. The landscape behind him was exactly the same. And in front it seemed to stretch on indefinitely, with no sign of any change.

He stopped and tried to find out what exactly it was that was bothering him. Was it something in himself? What had he been thinking about when the odd feeling stole over him? He couldn't remember. He had been at peace, contented, empty.

That was what had attracted him to this area, the emptiness of the place. The flatness of the sea, the almost equally flat and yet slightly inclined land, the long stretch of road running parallel with the coastline, and the sense of height that the cliffs gave, even though you couldn't see them from the road, for you were above them. But you knew they were there, you knew you were that much above sea level, and this avoided any sense of oppression that the flatness might otherwise have given.

And yet, oppression was precisely what he had become aware of at that particular moment. As if he had walked into an invisible cloud. Or a miasma. He looked up at the sky. Nothing there to explain the phenomenon – just a pale, even grey, from north to south, from east to west. A grey so light that you could almost have called it white, as if the sun were about to break through at any moment. A grey full of promise.

He stood still for a moment, puzzled and discomfited by this strange sensation. Should he go on? He certainly hadn't meant to turn back yet. He was looking forward to a good long walk. Not just for the pleasure of being out in the open air, away from the city, but also as a way of getting the feel of this particular stretch of the coast.

He decided that it would be silly to allow himself to be deflected by an indefinable sensation, and strode forward, faster than before. After all, it probably had nothing to do with his surroundings. And yet he couldn't rid himself of the conviction that this feeling had come to him from the outside, from the place itself.

He now turned his thoughts to the other, more important decision he still had to make. He liked the village, he liked the house – and when you work at home that's a very important consideration. Not only your personal happiness, but your work itself can be affected if you and the house don't, as it were, get on.

Right from the start, on his first visit last week, he had felt a great sense of affinity with the little house.

Now that the previous owners had left and taken all their things with them he had a better idea of how it would look with his own furniture in it. And he had plenty of time to examine the place thoroughly, for they had told him at the solicitor's office that he needn't return the keys till five o'clock. He had spent most of the morning pottering about the house – pottering mentally, that is, moving his furniture about effortlessly, putting up a shelf here, removing a door there. His fingers were itching to get started on the real thing.

The big bedroom upstairs he would turn into his study; the little one at the back would do all right for sleeping in. He'd worked out that there was enough space in the front room for most of his books. Any surplus, (and in time there certainly would be a surplus), he could accommodate on shelves in the corridors. He smiled as he visualized himself twenty years hence, edging his way from one room to another through corridors lined on both sides with books.

Funny, he thought, how books generate books. But then, if you're a lexicographer, that's your raw material. After all, if I were a carpenter my raw material would take up a lot more space. And, what's more, it would constantly have to be renewed. But it's different with words – you can use them and use them and use them and yet your stock never diminishes. Like the widow's cruse.

Suddenly he realized that he had completely shaken off the queer feeling. He seemed to have walked right out of the threatening area. He now tried to dismiss the thought of it from his mind and concentrate on the decision before him.

The house, he was sure, would be all right, just what

he wanted. But he also had to think about the village and the general situation. He had a wide choice before him. More or less anywhere along the east coast of Scotland would do, as long as it was within driving distance of a university library.

He'd had a 'wee daunder' round the village in the morning, and he liked the look of it. One of those rather austere Scottish villages strung out along the top of a cliff, braced against the east wind. Nothing fancy or picturesque about it; but good, strong, well built houses, and enough shops to see to his day-to-day needs. A sober village – well, architecturally, at least. He had no information as to the mores of its inhabitants. He liked the plain, down-to-earth, enduring look of the houses. Nothing here to attract the tourist, he noted with approbation. Their cars would file past his house (his, already?) in their quest for the bonnier bits of Bonnie Scotland, but they wouldn't stop. He'd be able to look down on to their roofs as they slid past. Then he would have a long, refreshing look out to sea, and turn back to his work.

He sighed with satisfaction as he contemplated the peaceful picture, then turned his gaze once again on his actual surroundings. Perhaps it was time to think about turning back. He must have done about three miles already. Leaving the road, he walked over to the cliffs, from where he could look down to a rocky shoreline. Here and there the odd sandy cove, most of them cut off from each other by stretches of rock. And then the sea, nothing but the sea. And gulls, of course, lots of gulls, wheeling and shrieking, flashing white against the grey of the sea.

He'd be able to learn all about sea birds, he thought. He knew their names – wonderful names full of distance and sea spray – shearwater, petrel, albatross, cormorant, kittiwake, guillemot, auk. Oh yes, he knew their names all right. But for the last few years he had been increasingly bothered by the fact that so much of his knowledge was theoretical, *in vacuo*. When faced with the real thing he often found he couldn't give it a name. And when he did find out it was often only to discover that he was already familiar with the word; he just hadn't got round to matching the word with the thing.

He was beginning to suspect that the unlettered churl who knows the thing but not its correct name was perhaps in a better state than he was, with all the floating, unattached words he had at his command. His natural impulse was to refute this heresy. Words were real too, weren't they? Every bit as real as a window or a walrus. This internal argument usually ended with the confession that probably it was best to be familiar with both the thing and the name. It was part of his project, in moving out to the country, to establish a firmer relationship between the thing and the word.

He turned his back on the sea and was about to start walking back to the road, when it occurred to him that he could follow the cliff edge back to the village. It would take longer, of course, because the coastline was irregular, with some deep inlets and some far promontories. But he had plenty of time. It was only ten miles from the village to the little town where he had to hand in the keys. If he left the house at twenty to five he'd be all right.

A great sense of relief flooded over him as he set off along the cliff edge, and at first he couldn't account for this at all. Suddenly he stopped in his tracks. Coward, he told himself, and strode firmly back to the road. If he couldn't face going through that disturbing area again, he might as well give up all thought of settling here.

For this walk was one of the main attractions. He had visions of himself walking along here every day, in all weathers, becoming familiar with the place in its different aspects – spring, summer, autumn, winter. He would be here, getting to know it, as he had never known any piece of land before. Cementing the relationship between thing and word. He thought of the elderly Kant going out for his walk every day in life, so punctual and so predictable that people set their watches by him. Well, he certainly didn't contemplate anything quite so rigidly programmed, though he did intend to have a daily walk, and felt sure that this would be the chosen direction most days.

But if his high, open walk was to have a menacing patch in it . . .

There were no landmarks in this monotonous landscape. It would be difficult to know when exactly he'd got to the ominous spot. Just as well, of course. That would make it a fairer test. No question of getting all hot and bothered just because he knew he'd reached the danger spot. As it was, he might go through it without noticing anything. Then he could forget about the whole thing, assuming that the discomfort he had felt was a purely subjective matter, and had nothing to do with the place.

After all, it wasn't as if he was sensitive to that sort of thing, or given to intuitions or anything of the kind. He sighed as he remembered how cheerfully he had seen his mother on to the plane that a few minutes later was to plummet into the Irish Sea, with the loss of all passengers and crew. No, he hadn't had the slightest premonition.

That sort of thing was more in Joan's line of country. She was almost a sensitive, some might say. He and Joan had been lovers for years, and he had assumed that nothing would change this. But eventually she had decided that her career must come first, and she had gone off to London.

It was at this point that Calum suddenly realized there was nothing to tie him to Edinburgh any longer. He could do his work just as well in the country, provided he had reasonable access to a library. And was it not time that he too had a change?

As he walked back now he smiled as he remembered the thrill with which he had contemplated this total upheaval in his life. Rather to his surprise, he had come to his decision quickly and painlessly. But he had made it very clear to himself that he was not going to hurry over his choice. He would spend some time looking round, seeing places, examining houses. And he was not going to let himself be won over by some attractive detail in an otherwise unsuitable house.

That flat in York, for instance, some years ago. It had a *For Sale* sign in the window, one floor up, in the Shambles. A very old, half-timbered house, that was one of the things he liked about it. But the other, the thing that nearly sent him straight along to the house agent's, was the floor, which was at least fifteen degrees off the horizontal. This appealed to his imagination so compellingly that he had to reason with himself very sternly before he was prepared to give up the idea. What on earth was he going to do in York? And besides, a floor with a fifteen-degree incline was hardly a guarantee of structural stability or domestic convenience.

But he knew he was like that about houses. Any odd little quirk, any unusual or attractive feature, and he was won over. So he was being very circumspect. He reflected with satisfaction that he had resisted the blandishments of a twisty little staircase in an otherwise equally unsuitable house further up the coast. And as for that adorable little turret in the house he had seen yesterday . . .

His self-congratulation was cut short by a sudden, intense feeling of unease. At first it took the form of a suspicion that there was someone behind him. In spite of his conviction that this was not in fact the case, he was unable to stop himself from turning round. No-one, as expected. Since setting out he hadn't seen a single human being, apart from one or two car drivers. The road, he knew from a study of the map, only led to a little hamlet some four or five miles further on, and one or two isolated farms, so there was very little traffic on it. At the present moment he could neither see nor hear any signs of life. What then was it that made him feel so uncomfortable?

He walked on, trying to convince himself that what he was feeling at the moment was simply the memory of his former disquiet. This time at least he had a clear recollection of what he had been thinking of when the trouble fell upon him. He'd been patting himself on the back for having resisted the temptations of a quirky little staircase and an absurd little turret. Nothing to feel uncomfortable about, and nothing to do with the memory of his previous odd sensation. He'd forgotten all about that.

In spite of a desire to hurry and get past the bad bit, he forced himself to stand still. He wanted to analyse what he felt, to come up with some sort of definition.

Apprehension, was that the word? Or rather, some indefinable kind of dread? And a touch of disgust as well, as if there were something hidden and filthy about the place. And a deep, almost overwhelming sense of personal inadequacy, when faced with this indefinable dread.

He stood there till he felt he could bear it no longer, and then walked on as fast as he could. It took a great effort of will to keep himself from running.

After a few minutes he felt he had walked clear of the radius of the evil, and relaxed his pace. He spent the rest of the time till he got back to the village trying to think of some possible explanation. Had someone been murdered on that lonely spot? A battle fought, perhaps? Or was there some perfectly normal explanation connected with the natural world? Radon, wasn't that the name? The radioactive gas that some rocks emit. He had no idea whether one could actually feel the presence of radon. Nor did he know whether it had ever been discovered along the east coast of Scotland. Cornwall, he rather fancied that was where it was supposed to be found, coming from the rocks. Well, there were plenty of rocks here – the cliffs, the whole shoreline.

He was still feeling rather shaken when he got back to the house. He had decided he couldn't possibly come and live here, so near this inexplicable threat.

But as soon as he was indoors he fell victim to the seductions of the house. Wherever he looked he saw his own books, his own furniture, his own crockery neatly and comfortably housed. He stood in the kitchen and remembered how he had enjoyed his picnic lunch there only a few hours ago, sitting on the old-fashioned kitchen chair that had been left behind, using the draining-board as a table, looking out onto what would be his own little garden.

The thought of leaving this house that he had never actually lived in filled him with nostalgia. How could he bear not to come and live in it now that he had eaten a meal in it, now that he had gone out for a walk and come back to it as to his home? And this time he knew that his attachment to the house was a perfectly reasonable one. This house was in all respects suitable for him. He hadn't fallen in love with some bizarre feature. There was nothing at all bizarre about it. It was a nice, solid, homely, comfortable little place, just the very thing he was looking for. Only . . .

Desolately he went up to what was to have been his study, and stood gazing out to sea. The sensible thing, of course, would be to make inquiries. But who do you ask, and what do you ask about, in such a nebulous situation? And anyway, even if he did find some explanation of the phenomenon, it would still be there, wouldn't it? It would still pounce upon him every time he passed, spoiling his walk, filling him with dread. And even if there was nothing there, even if it could be proved to him that it was nothing but his own imagination, where would that get him? It would still be his imagination, and it would set the horror upon him every time he passed. And how did he know that it would always be in the same place? Perhaps it would creep up on him in his little garden, perhaps it would steal into his bedroom and make his nights hideous with fear.

Suddenly he remembered about the time, and looked at his watch. Ten to five! He would never make it. Without even stopping to collect his picnic things he rushed out, locked the door and leapt into the car. Then he drove like a maniac and reached the town a few minutes after five.

He had been so engrossed in his dangerous driving that he still hadn't come to any conclusion about the house. He rushed into the office and found the secretary standing with the office keys in her hand.

'I'm afraid Mr McGill's left,' she said. 'He's a very punctual gentleman.'

'I'm terribly sorry. Watch stopped.' It wasn't true, but how could he possibly tell her the real cause of his delay? 'Here you are, the keys,' he said as he handed them over.

'And what am I to say to Mr McGill?'

'Tell him . . . ' he paused, still undecided. 'Tell him I'm taking it.'

Three weeks later he was moving in, excited, slightly alarmed, and rather smug. He had faced his challenge, he hadn't allowed himself to be intimidated by the unknown. He would have felt most dissatisfied with himself if he had called off just because of that mysterious something in the air. He would have felt he was betraying the dear little house that had welcomed him so warmly. He was now more convinced than ever that this was the right place for him and his possessions.

He had a lovely time putting up shelves, moving furniture about to get everything just where it wanted to be, getting his beloved books just where he needed them most. It was one of the happiest periods of his life.

For the first few weeks he didn't go near the suspect area. Just little walks, he told himself – he'd still got too much to do in the house. Besides, he wanted to explore all the walks round about the village. Even if he did decide that the cliff walk was to be the regular one, he could only make an informed choice if he knew what else was available.

In the end, however, he ran out of excuses for not going that way, and set off one sunny afternoon, determined to tackle the enemy. Whatever it was, he had to admit that it was still there. That, or else his expectation; which, for practical purposes, came to much the same thing. But he was able to get through the bad patch with commendable composure.

On his way back he decided to skirt the obstacle, and struck further inland well before reaching the danger zone, till he found the main road, which at this point ran parallel. This brought him back, unscathed, to the village. Altogether he was fairly satisfied with the experiment. He felt that he and his unknown antagonist had come to some sort of *modus vivendi*.

After he had got properly settled in, his friends started coming to see him in his new home. He was anxious to discuss his problem with some of them. At the same time he wanted to know whether they reacted spontaneously to the spot, so he said nothing beforehand. Nobody seemed to feel anything.

Calum, reassured, came to the conclusion that there must just be something about the configuration of that particular bit of road that affected him in some special way. He must be more sensitive to the hidden influences of place than he had imagined. But since no-one else noticed anything he felt he could assume that the matter was of little importance. He certainly wasn't going to let it spoil his pleasure in his new home. He wasn't even going to let it deflect him from the walk he had chosen that very first day as his regular outing.

So most days he set off with determination and walked right through the bad patch. On his way back he sometimes skirted it, sometimes braved it. He just came to look on it as one of those bothersome things you have to do every day, like getting up, or shaving, or doing the washing up.

He had been in the cottage for more than a year when Joan paid her first visit to Scotland since going to live in London. She came to spend a couple of days with him and inspect his new home. He found her rather changed – livelier and more talkative than before. She liked his new home, and agreed that he had made a very good move. She perfectly understood the way he had felt he was being drawn to the house, and could see that he was very happy there.

She was interested in everything, wanted to know how he spent his free time, and insisted on doing his daily walk with him the very day she arrived. He wondered whether to tell her about the odd patch, but decided to do as he had with his other friends, and not say anything beforehand. It would be interesting if she noticed anything; but he felt this was most unlikely. By now he was sure that, however real the thing might be to him, it had no existence for other people. He had come to look on it as the inevitable counterbalance to the powerful forces that attracted him to this place.

He knew he would be able to discuss all this with Joan without any fear of her pooh-poohing the whole thing. Joan took an interest in corn circles and ESP and other controversial phenomena. But he wouldn't mention the matter till afterwards, after she had walked through the bad patch and he had seen her reaction – if any.

They set off that afternoon. Joan was in good spirits, and delighted to be in the country. They chatted about this and that, and how wonderful it was to feel the fresh sea breeze.

As they approached the danger zone Calum wondered whether she would feel the sea breeze any less fresh in a moment or two.

Soon he began to notice the familiar sense of oppression, but did his best to go on talking as usual.

During a pause he heard her voice, faint and as if far away.

'I think I'd like to turn back,' she was saying.

She was standing still, looking very white, and he saw that she was shaking slightly.

'Joan, dearest, you look frozen. Here, take my jacket.' In a moment he had taken it off and wrapped it round her. Then he put his arm round her shoulder and they turned and started walking back.

They still had a little way to go before he knew they would be clear of the evil influence, when Joan gave a little cry, broke from him and started running towards the cliff. She had moved off so quickly that it took him a moment to catch up with her and pull her away from the edge, which at this point was not far from the road. She was weeping hysterically most of the way back, but managed to compose herself and return his jacket just before entering the village.

A little later as they sat by the fire over a cup of tea, she said:

'I'm sorry, that was a very foolish way to behave. I don't know what came over me.'

'No, it's I who should apologize. I'll explain, as far as

I can explain, in a minute. But tell me first, what did you feel? What was it that upset you?'

'I don't quite know.' Joan gazed at the fire for a while. 'A sort of dread, I suppose you could call it. And a sort of immense, cosmic despair. I can't describe it any better than that. Just a sort of unbearableness.'

They spent a long time discussing the problem. Joan agreed with him that the distressing feelings evoked by that particular spot must be the debit side of the powerful attraction that the rest of the area, and the house in particular, had for him.

Calum had a restless night. He was worried about Joan's reaction to the strange influence of his now familiar trouble spot, for she was evidently still very shaken. In addition, for the first time, he had proof that the whole business was not a figment of his imagination. For the first time since his original decision to take the house, he found himself wondering whether he had done the right thing.

At long last he fell asleep. When he woke up he felt as if he had hardly slept at all. It was daylight, and he could see Joan lying beside him. Her eyes were open.

'What time is it?' he asked sleepily.

'Six o'clock. Go to sleep. It's too early to get up.'

Calum laid a hand on her bare shoulder. He had a vague idea of making love, but fell asleep instead.

When he woke up he saw that Joan had gone. He remembered that she was an early riser, and decided that she was probably downstairs making breakfast.

He would get up, go downstairs and be greeted by the heavenly smells of hot toast and freshly ground coffee. He was still tired, but this at least would be worth getting up for. He dressed quickly and decided he would shave later. Then he went downstairs.

No smell of toast, no hot coffee, and no Joan. For a moment he was puzzled. Then suddenly he knew.

He grabbed the car keys, rushed out and drove furiously along the cliff road, looking for the slight figure in the red anorak. When he got to the spot where Joan had broken away from him the previous afternoon he pulled the steering wheel round and drove towards the cliff. His knees were trembling as he got out of the car and advanced to the very edge.

The tide was coming in and the water was beginning to lap gently round the outstretched hand of the red-clad figure that lay face downwards on the rocks.

The inquest found that the cause of death was suicide while the balance of the mind was disturbed. No-one was prepared to say what had disturbed the balance.

What Calum's friends were prepared to say, and did say with some insistence, was that he couldn't possibly think of staying on in that place.

But Calum refused to leave. Joan was dead, and nothing could bring her back. Whether he went away or stayed on would make no difference to that. But going away, somehow, struck him as a rather callous thing to do. After all, he had, albeit unwittingly, lured poor Joan to her death in this place. It was irrational of him, of course; but he felt he really owed it to her to stay. How could he abandon her now?

He remembered how she had agreed with him that he seemed to be very finely attuned to this particular house and its immediate surroundings. Surely she would have preferred him to stay? As he saw it, the forces of both good and evil exerted an unusually strong pull in this area on those sensitive enough to feel them. Perhaps, with Joan's death, the evil thing had been placated.

But he wasn't going to try and find out, just in case. He stayed on, he continued to take his regulation walk, but he skirted the threatening area every time.

After a while he got to be quite fond of the inland route. But as soon as he got past the danger zone he would turn seawards again, back to his beloved coastal road, with the sea and the sky and the flat, tilted land for company.

33

A nation without beggars?

'Ai, perdoni!'

The beggar looked up at the young man who had almost tripped over him. This one at least had apologized. Most of them didn't. Not that everyone tripped over him; but quite a few did, and this was inevitable. If your pitch isn't in the way, you just won't be noticed. Nobody goes about looking for a beggar to give a few coppers to.

In the narrow street beside the ancient church of Santa Maria del Mar, the pavement was always busy. You got a few kicks, mostly unintentional, but you also got quite a few coins, on a good day.

'Here you are!'

The young man had turned back and was offering him something.

Ferran held out his hand to receive the coins. As he did so he noticed that the boy was looking at him earnestly.

That's odd, he thought. Most people look the other way when they give you something, as if they were ashamed. And so they should be, when you think of how much most of them have, and how little they give. All they give is a

few coppers they don't need, that's all. And they give it
without love.

But this young man, why had he looked in that way?
And why had he come back, when he must have been
quite a way off?

Well, anyway, he's gone now, and won't come back
a second time. I'll probably never see him again. I just
wish I'd looked at him a little more closely.

He did come back, the very next day. He walked right
up to Ferran and stopped. For a moment Ferran thought
he was going to ask him something. But all he said was
'*Tingui*,' as he held out his hand and gave him some
more coins. Then he turned and walked on.

This time Ferran had a really good look at him. Late
teens, medium height, with a slim, wiry frame; dark, like
most of his fellow Catalans; and the eyes, yes, the eyes,
with their soft, glowing intensity . . . Eyes that looked at
you as if they loved you.

Ferran spent the rest of the day sitting on the pavement,
leaning against the venerable wall of the old church,
thinking of those eyes and the message they seemed to
convey, longing to see them again, knowing that this was
completely out of his power. Unless the youth came again,
there was no way Ferran could hope to see him. He didn't
know the boy's name, where he lived, where he worked or
studied. For the thousandth time he cursed the impotence
of his situation. For what could a lame beggar do to find
out more about a stranger? Over the years he had got used
to the limitations the Civil War had imposed on him; and
while he still had spells of straining at the bit, longing to
do something to better his lot, the original urgency of the
desire had died down.

Pretty nearly everything in his life, he reflected, had died down – fears, terrors, hopes, affection, laughter. All these had become mere shadows in a life with no changes, with nothing good or bad to be expected any longer. Yes, that was it – no expectations. You take what comes. Not exactly gratefully, for you've not much to be grateful for beyond the knowledge that things could be even worse.

When evening came he got ready to leave. First of all he unrolled the trouser leg that he kept pulled up during what he thought of as working hours. The stump of his leg, which had been severed just below the knee, was one of his assets, proof that he really had a severe disability, that he couldn't possibly carry out a day's work – not the only type of work available for a man with no influence and no position in society.

Then he collected his few bits and pieces; his cap, with the usual few coins in it, the tin box with the remains of the day's supply of food, a large, filthy canvas bag into which all the smaller things were put, and finally, his crutch.

Getting into an upright position was always a struggle. This was when he really felt he could do with a little help. Most people ignored his efforts. Just occasionally someone would lend a steadying hand. But this only happened when a passer-by as poor and ragged as himself was near.

This time there was no-one in sight when he began the operation. He shuffled forward till he was sitting on the edge of the pavement, with his one foot resting on the roadway. Then he placed the end of his crutch in the gutter. Holding on to the upright crutch, he swung himself on to his knees and pulled himself up. Resting on his foot, he got the padded end of the crutch under the opposite arm and was ready to walk, with his canvas bag slung over his free shoulder.

As he went through the tricky operation he thought once again of those two compassionate eyes, and imagined their owner there beside him, helping him up, walking along beside him through the narrow shabby streets of old Barcelona.

Next day the devil, expectation, took hold of him again. On both the previous days the boy had appeared just before eight o'clock. Ferran couldn't take his eyes off the direction from which he had come.

And once again he arrived.

This time he came straight to Ferran and asked:

'Do you mind if I talk to you?'

'Go ahead.'

'If I ask a few questions?'

Ferran nodded.

The young man squatted down beside the beggar.

'You were in the Civil War, I suppose?'

'Yes.'

'Which side?'

'Which does it look like? I wouldn't be here begging if I'd been on the winning side, would I?'

'And where do you come from?'

'Ripoll.'

'Oh!'

The young man looked disappointed.

'Why are you asking?'

'Because my father disappeared during the war, just before I was born, so I never knew him. But I've seen photos, and you look so like him – at least so like what I imagine he would look like now. And I thought—'

'You thought you'd found your father. Very funny.' Ferran gave a harsh laugh. 'Well, you've had a lucky escape, haven't you? Who would want to have a father like this? Maimed, ragged, dirty? A beggar?'

He was bitterly disappointed that this young man's interest in him had evidently been founded on a misconception. Now no doubt he would straighten up again and go on his way.

Instead the boy gave him a troubled look and asked:

'Did you know your father? Was he there when you were a child?'

'Yes, he was there, the old bugger. I'd just as well have done without him, if I'd been given the choice.'

'Ah, but we're not given the choice. And all my life I've longed for this father, and it would have been so wonderful to find him, even if he was . . . ' The boy stopped and looked away, awkwardly.

'Even if he was a stinking old beggar with only one foot?' The ferocity of Ferran's tone showed how much he resented the implied offence. That loving look he had seen in the boy's eyes, that was for the missing father, not for him.

The boy was looking really upset.

'I'm sorry, I didn't mean . . . ' He stood up and made a gesture of helplessness with his hands. 'There's nothing more to be said, is there?'

The beggar shrugged, then said:

'So you don't need to keep on passing this way, do you?'

'Well, it's the nearest way to the *acadèmia* I go to in

the Rambla. But I can go round the other side of the church, if you'd rather.'

Ferran looked up suddenly.

'No. Keep on passing. And by the way, what's your name?

'Andreu Ribes.'

'Right, Andreu. You can go now.'

After Andreu had left, Ferran sat very still, staring straight ahead, so absorbed that he didn't even notice whether any of the passers-by were dropping coins into his upturned cap.

Next day, as soon as Andreu appeared, Ferran signed to him to come and speak to him.

'*Bon dia, jove.*'

'*Bon dia tingui.*'

'What's the name of that *acadèmia* you go to?'

'Acadèmia Soler.'

'Oh! So it's not the one.'

'Not what one?'

'Never mind. I'll tell you some other time.'

Ferran was eighteen years old. He had left school and started at university. And in the evenings he walked down from the family flat in the *eixample* to the Acadèmia Pedralbes to study English. In a few years he would have a degree in law and would be properly qualified to join in the great task of helping to draw his country out of the dark ages. More schools, libraries, museums . . . It was going to be a more open society, with less poverty, no injustice. The Republic would rid the land of all the medieval ideas and abuses that had crippled it for centuries.

Life was a glorious journey, moving forward into new,

vibrant landscapes. His father, a successful lawyer in the provincial city of Ripoll, had decided to move his family to the capital, Barcelona, in order to be nearer the centre of political and intellectual life. Every evening, after he had finished his classes at the university, Ferran would stroll down the Rambla to his evening class, enjoying the varied life of the city – the crowds, the traffic, the blaze of colour at all the flower stalls, and the combined noise of the people shouting and laughing, the hooting of horns and the screech of brakes, and the singing of tiny birds in their tiny cages set out on the pavement for sale.

Life, life, he would say to himself as he strolled, this is life – exciting, varied, full of possibilities. And he would look at the pretty girls, at the expensive cars, and think, all this is waiting for me. All I have to do is walk right into it, just saunter along this sunlit avenue, with its tall plane trees for shade and its crowds for company. Friends, I'm on my way.

After the outbreak of the Civil War life became more serious and even more exciting. This glorious future that he saw for himself and his whole country, he was going to have to fight for it. He left for the front full of hope, eager to savour all the new experiences that the war was to bring. His companions – factory workers, bus drivers, shop assistants, peasants – taught him how privileged his life had been so far. Well, never mind, he wasn't going to feel guilty about it, for was he not fighting for the side that would wipe out all injustices?

The life was hard, but he enjoyed it. Sometimes they advanced, sometimes they retreated. Near the end of the war, when retreating seemed to be all they were now able to do, an enemy bullet shot his left leg to pieces just above the ankle. There was no way of saving the foot. He arrived back in Barcelona the day before Franco's advancing forces took over.

The army lorry that had brought him dropped him off with his two crutches in Plaça Catalunya, the very heart of the city. It was a long drag uphill to his home, and he wondered what he would find there, for the city seemed strangely empty, and showed many gaping wounds where the bombs had done their work.

At last he got to the luxurious apartment block. He was seen by the *portera* in her little cabin.

'*Ai senyoret Ferran, és vostè?*'

'Yes, it's me, Felissa. What's left of me. Are my parents at home?'

The woman burst into tears and told him that his parents had that very morning joined the endless procession heading for France, convinced that Barcelona was about to fall to Franco's army.

'And the neighbours?'

'They've left too, every one of them. There's no-one left in Barcelona except for a few folks like us, too poor to travel, too poor to escape.'

Ferran never saw his people again. He set off to follow them, but found no means of transport. Hobbling along on his crutches, he was soon overtaken by the victorious *franquistas* and imprisoned for his allegiance to the Republic. When at last he was released he found out that his mother had died on the bitter journey into exile, and that his father had reached France, but only survived for a couple of years.

Ferran had learned enough about what things were like now in Spain to know he had little to look forward to with his freedom. The situation turned out to be even worse than he had expected. All doors were closed to him. The only thing a man in his position could hope for was to earn a meagre living by labouring. And who would employ a man with a missing foot? By now he had learned to get about with the help of only one crutch; but you can't carry bricks or mix cement or even sweep the streets unless you have two hands *and* two feet available.

In a way taking up a beggar's life suited his mood. It was the ultimate, unanswerable negation of all he had hoped for in life, and seemed a fitting image for what his country had now become. The years went past in a sort of numb, bleak acceptance that this was all life had to offer. Sometimes he thought of his youthful dreams of a better land for all his countrymen, and of the happy, carefree days, sauntering through his beloved Barcelona, with nothing more on his mind than his studies. But it was all so far away, so far, that he found it hard to believe such a life had ever existed.

But of course it had, and it was still going on for some people. He saw the young men and women going to their classes, carrying their books, but he still found it hard to believe in this life full of hope and a future . . .

It was the word *acadèmia* that Andreu had used – that was what suddenly got through to him. It was like a knife cutting through the tissue of misery, poverty, lost hopes. The thick wadding of indifference he had built up over the years of catastrophe had been pierced. He wanted to know more, to feel more, to hope once again, if not for himself, at least for the country he had so longed to serve as a young man. Yes, as a young man like this Andreu, with his glowing eyes and his gentle manner.

So from then on, whenever Andreu passed, he would crouch down beside the beggar and, prompted by Ferran's questions, he would talk about his studies and his companions, and how hard they were all working.

'All of them?'

Ferran was remembering what it was like a generation ago.

'*All* of them?' he repeated.

'Well, no, not quite all. Some are just having fun. But most are working hard. They really want to succeed.'

'For what? What are they aiming at? A good job that will get them a flashy car and enough money to build their little *torre* by the sea to spend the summer in?'

'Of course that's what a lot of them want. But some of us are aiming slightly higher. Or lower, by their standards. Anyway some of us are hoping to do something for the people of this country in general – schools, libraries, hospitals. We want to see a nation where no-one has to live like you.'

'A nation without beggars?'

'Yes, that's it. That summarizes the whole ideal.'

Nearly every day they would have a little chat. Ferran was always keen to hear about what Andreu was studying, what the classes were like, how things had changed inside the classroom. He would have liked to discuss the curriculum in more detail – what textbooks were they using, how much written work did they have to do, what was the expected standard? But he was careful never to let Andreu see that he knew so well what they were talking about, that he himself had been in exactly the same situation, with the same hopes and aims, a generation earlier.

It would have been too cruel. It was better to leave the young man his hopes and his aspirations. A nation without beggars! Yes, a wonderful dream. And who knows, who knows? Not even a dictator can live for ever.

34

Graffiti

As soon as I got into the kitchen Mum told me to get out of her way.

'I only wanted a Coke!'

'There aren't any left. You had the last one half an hour ago.'

'Get some more, then.'

And that's when she started screaming at me. Get them yourself, time you started paying for your own bloody Cokes. And all the rest of it.

Hell, I'm only at school, where am I supposed to get the money?

Dad was sitting in the living room, reading the paper. I switched on the telly and turned it up loud. He roared at me to put the damn thing off. I didn't bother. Just walked out of the house, leaving him and the telly roaring at each other. Funny, really, but I suppose I'll pay for it when I get back.

If I go back.

Yes, *if*.

After all, I don't need to go back. I'm a free agent.

Sixteen years of age, sound in wind and limb, at least average intelligence.

Christ, the world's full of kids my age who are out on their own. I don't *need* to go back. I don't *need* to be dependent.

That's what gets to me, really, this having to be dependent all the time, having to do what they say. I'm an individual, right? I can do as I please.

And right now I could do with a Coke. Supermarket over there, I'll go and get one. Hang on, though . . . Have I got enough money? Two p, five p . . . Is that all? Won't get a lot of Coke for seven p, will I?

So, what can I do? I'm a free agent, right? What are my options?

I can go to a friend and borrow some money. And then what? Then I get my Coke and I drink it. And then what? Yes, exactly, what happens after that? What does a free agent do then, with no money? And owing the price of a Coke?

I can do without the Coke, of course, that's another option. Only, it's not much fun, doing without, even when you're not thirsty. And I *am* thirsty. So that's even less fun. And I'd still have no money.

Or I can go home and nag Mum till she gets me some Coke or gives me the money to go and get it myself. Fine, I get the Coke that way. But where's the free agent in that scenario? I'd be depending on her, wouldn't I? And I'd *still* have no money.

Trapped!

Suddenly I want to run amok. I mean, I know what it feels like, to want to run, and yell, and break things and hit

people, even kill people, yes, kill them, kill, kill . . . Ex-
ter-min-ate, I could exterminate the lot of them.

Choking, just choking with rage and frustration. Violence rising in me, ready to explode, to shatter and
smash and lash out . . . I want to scream and scream
and scream . . .

And then I see this wall. A great, big, blank wall on
the side of a building. Whitewashed. And it's like a great,
white peace coming over me.

And I think, what I really want is a big, big aerosol
spray, and a ladder to help me get up high, and then
start writing. Cover the wall with graffiti, cover the wall
with all the rage and frustration and disappointment and
contempt inside me. Tell them what I think of them all.
Tell them how I hate this web of chains they've caught
me in – all their rules and regulations and moral standards and social values, their religion and their psychology
and all their bloody rights and wrongs.

Chained, chained, I'm chained by all the rules of the
game. It's *their* game, they invented it, they made up the
rules, they force me to play it. But I never asked to play
it, I never asked – I never even asked to come.

I can just see me standing on that ladder, with an aerosol
can in my hand, stretching up, up, to write that first letter,
that F as big as myself. Writing words so enormous, so
monstrous, so unthinkable – words *they* don't even know.
Me, standing up on the ladder, pouring out all those words
they won't let me use, all those things they won't let me
say, all the tangle of chains and string and red tape they've
crammed into my brain to stop it from thinking.

Pouring the lot out, till my brain starts working freely
again, a splendid, beautiful machine, moving smoothly,

quietly, full of purpose and energy, free from all the loops and snags and knots they've jammed into it with all their teaching, their warnings, their drills and directions and indoctrinations.

And once I've flung all that on to the wall, turned it into screaming graffiti, with all that empty space inside me, then I'll know what to do, I'll know where I am, I'll know *who* I am.

I can't do it, of course. I haven't even got enough to buy the aerosol spray. I haven't got a ladder. And I haven't got a blank wall. Perhaps I haven't even got the vocabulary. I'd have to invent new words, violent, shocking, scandalous, outrageous words. Words like debonking, lecherboob, condomania, spreadshit, arsinogenic . . .

Well, I can have a nice time inventing words, but what then? What's the point if I can't do anything with them?

Nothing, nothing, nothing . . .

So I just go home again, dreaming of graffiti, but go home because the chains hold me too fast – and because I'm thirsty.

'Oh, you're back are you? Thought you'd walked out on us for good.'

On my way to my room I look into the kitchen, and see six cans of Coke on the table. I take one, pull the ring, and start drinking straight from the can. Mum hates that, but she says nothing. This time, she says nothing. Don't know why. Anyway, I can feel her anger, her disapproval, and it's just as bad as if she'd yelled at me. Self-control, they call it. Just another of their bloody weapons. Makes them feel superior; and you can't even answer back, because they haven't said a thing.

In my room I have a good look round. No blank walls, no space for graffiti. Anyway, *my* room isn't the place for it. It's got to be one of *their* places.

After the meal, when they're both settled in front of the telly, I get my mapping pen and the Indian ink. I get a chair and stand on it, and I start writing, above the kitchen door, just along the top of the frame. So small they'll never see it. But it's there, *I* know it's there. My graffiti – *Fuck the lot of you.*

35

Monte Pardo

From a distance the Monte Pardo looks imposing, like
some vast, oddly shaped building, towering high above
the city. Row upon row of ornate galleries seem to stretch
from one end of the huge mass to the other, each shorter
than the one below, for the whole structure has the shape
of an enormous beehive.

As the observer approaches he sees that no two levels
are alike; and each gallery is divided into a long row of
small, totally dissimilar squares.

The effect is of the most intricate beauty and flamboy-
ant originality, both pattern and colour working together
to form this unique monument. What is it, building or
hill?

It is both.

Close at hand the fantastic vision turns out to be one of
the many hills on the outskirts of the city. But the lush
vegetation that covers the other *montes* has been stripped
off by the rash of hovels that make up the streets, now
no longer seen as galleries, of this immense shanty town.
Some of these *barracas* have, in fact, been carved out of

the soil of the hillside. These are the best, for some of them have been dug so deep into the side of the hill that they boast a second room – a room with no view, with rough gravel walls, but cool, and quiet. A good room to sleep in, a good room to die in. Away from the noise and the dust and the promiscuity of the other, more public, room.

But it is only the aristocrats of the community who have this second room, and only the more desirable residences that are dug out of the hill. The others have nothing but the bare hillside as the inner wall, with the rest of the structure made up of the detritus spawned by the city – car windscreens, planks, pieces of plywood, of Formica, of sheet metal, of cardboard even – the latter in need of renewal after every heavy rain. Ragged curtains of every conceivable fabric and colour fill the gaps, where the owner has run short of more durable materials.

These are the elements that make up the bewilderingly varied and intricate pattern of the Monte Pardo – a pattern created by the fertile demands of chance and need.

The respectable inhabitants of the city prefer to turn their back on the Monte Pardo, try not to see it, doubly ashamed. It outrages both their sense of justice and their sense of propriety. Other cities may have slums, but they manage to hide them better. Such well concealed areas of infestation can be safely ignored, even forgotten. But the Monte Pardo proclaims its presence both by day and by night. For in the dark the whole mass twinkles with tiny, random lights, turned on and off in some unpredictable sequence, like a handful of capricious glow-worms scattered over the hill. And all day what looks like the oriental opulence of the decor draws the eyes unfailingly towards it, so that the visitor gazes in wonder and, finally understanding, murmurs:

'But how picturesque!'

There is a no-man's-land between the city proper and the Monte Pardo – a narrow belt of dismantled factories and disused warehouses. Gutted buildings where everything detachable has been removed and carried painfully up the hill, to fill some gap in the wall, to be turned into an unsteady table or an improvised flowerpot.

Nobody has ever lived in this deserted area, nobody has worked there for years. It serves as the security zone for the city, keeping the infection at bay. For the dwellers of the Monte this grey area is equally vital. It marks the limit of official interference. Once a *montepardeño* has crossed from the good side of the last inhabited street of the city proper into the wasteland on the other side, he knows he is safe from the police. Only after the most serious of offences will he be pursued beyond this neutral ground. But this happens rarely, and when it does there is a shoot-out, with losses on both sides.

And the city cries out that this cannot be allowed to continue, that the central government must interfere, must put a stop to this intolerable situation, burn the shacks, round up all their inhabitants, imprison them, deport them, shoot them, hang them . . .

But the privileged citizens know, even the most naive of them know, that this will never happen, that it never can happen, for it is they themselves who unendingly create the situation with their wealth. Their luxury is the magnet. And they can raze the Monte Pardo to the ground, but it will rise again, feeding on the superfluity of its neighbours. And the *montepardeños* will continue to raid the city, stealing whatever they can, for this is how they live. What else can they do? They cannot work, for no-one will employ them.

They are filthy, ignorant, idle, utterly unreliable – who would employ them? Set one of them to water your orchard, and he will make off with the fruit. Ask him to mend a chair, and he will leave the job half-done and slip away with his pockets full of whatever comes to hand. And don't leave any of your children unattended when one of those people is about, for you may never see the child again. Once they have hidden him away in that rabbit warren, who will ever find him?

The two worlds exist side by side, feeding on each other, like good and evil, for ever opposed, for ever linked. And there is a one-way traffic between them, for in the end all the unredeemable failures of the bright and wealthy city cross over to the Monte, and dig and scrape and tie and join till they have made some sort of shelter for themselves, where they can live, outcasts and intruders, till time incorporates them in their adopted community.

Like all other new visitors to the city, the Stranger was amazed and fascinated by the sight of the Monte Pardo. He stood at the balcony of his friend's flat and stared across at the colourful, elaborate structure in front of him.

'And you say it's a hill, just an ordinary hill, covered with these rows and rows of shacks?'

'Exactly. That's what it is.'

'Who lives there?'

'The damned.'

The Stranger turned again to the window, his eyes resting on the Monte Pardo. 'It's like some fantastic, oriental palace, too elaborate, too convoluted, too various in its decoration to be true. It's like a dream.'

'Yes, it is a dream. Our dream and our nightmare.'

'Tomorrow', said the Stranger, 'I must go and get a closer view.'

'You must not. It would be dangerous. I think you should control your curiosity.'

'It isn't curiosity. It's something deeper.'

The Stranger set off early the following morning, just before daybreak, drawn by an irresistible conviction that he must see this place at close quarters, that he had something to do there, something to learn there. The meeting was not to be avoided.

His route took him down a long, straight street that led from one of the fashionable districts overlooking the city, down into the centre and from there through the working-class area next to the no-man's-land at the foot of Monte Pardo. As he set out he could just see the mass of the Monte, silhouetted against the faint light in the eastern sky.

On either side he had blocks of luxury flats with their spacious entrance halls, and villas surrounded by big, well kept gardens. This sense of space was still there in the shopping centre, with its wide boulevards, its huge shop windows, some of them displaying only one item – an evening coat, a dinner set, a bed of the most elaborate workmanship with a rich, shimmering spread thrown over it. Space and plate glass and neon lighting, and the silence of very early morning.

Looking ahead, the Stranger could make out the dark mass of the Monte Pardo looming above the city, blocking the view, closing the way ahead. If you go forward, that's where you end up, at the foot of this monstrous mountain. You can only avoid it by turning aside, going back, running away from the confrontation.

The Stranger walked on through the morning stillness till he realized he must be getting near the street that divides the respectable citizens from the untouchables. He was now clear of the shopping centre, surrounded by tenement buildings and rows of small, working-class houses.

And then came the dividing line, so clear-cut, so explicit, it was almost obscene. A long, straight street, with shabby houses on one side and a desert of half-demolished factories on the other. And everywhere, complete silence.

The Stranger crossed the street and stepped into one of the narrow openings between two large, roofless buildings. In the half-light he had to tread carefully to avoid the rubbish and rubble that lay about.

Soon he could see he was very near the foot of the towering Monte. As he approached his goal the light seemed to be growing less, not more, in spite of the advancing daylight.

Far behind him in the distance he made out the cry of a security alarm; then, moments later, came the siren-screams of first one, and then several, police cars. One of those raids, he thought, and wondered whether he should turn back.

Instead, he stepped clear of the last of the disused factories, and found himself at the very foot of the Monte Pardo, on the lowest level of the parallel streets that made up what he had at first sight taken to be galleries.

The Stranger had seen hovels before. He was prepared

for the poverty and desolation that greeted him, for the
dirt and disorder and overcrowding. What he had never
before seen was this geometrical arrangement of shacks,
row upon row climbing neatly up the mountainside, as if
the whole thing had been planned from the very beginning.
Other shanty towns are haphazard, improvised, crowded
together without symmetry and without plan, the sponta-
neous response to personal or collective disaster, unfore-
seen, perhaps unforeseeable. But the regular, regimented
distribution of these bizarre little huts, with their wild
individuality so uniformly subjected to the overall design,
seemed to imply a predetermined pattern, a governing will
that only the spirit of evil itself could have decreed.

The first thing he noticed was the stench. To get into
any of the hovels you had to step across an open drain.
That seemed to be the full extent of the sanitation provided. The Stranger wondered what the mortality rate on
the Monte must be.

Then he noticed a difference in the quality of the
silence – a waiting quality, you might say, made up of
tiny, almost imperceptible sounds. From the nearest hut,
just a few paces away from where he stood, came a gentle
snoring. From a few streets above, a baby's cry, frightened
into silence by a woman's voice cursing angrily. Breathing, he felt; the whole hillside was breathing, quietly,
irregularly. It was a living stillness, quite different from
the empty silence of the warehouses he had just quitted.

Something moved at his feet, and he looked down. A
small child, two or three years old, had crawled out from
under the curtain that served as a door to the nearest hut.
The tiny creature was sitting in the doorway, her bare
little feet dangling over the edge of the drain, just clear

of the ordure. Only the top half of her body was clothed, in a filthy rag. Her hair was dark and unkempt, her face streaked with dirt, and her dark, glowing eyes were fixed on the Stranger with a mixture of curiosity and mistrust.

A moment later a deep growl emerged from the hut, and a man's hand appeared, grabbed the child roughly by the arm, and dragged her in behind the curtain.

The Stranger walked along the street, looking for some way of getting up to the higher levels. He had to go quite a distance, several hundred paces, before he found a break between two buildings. Access from one level to the next had apparently not been a high priority with the planners. When he came to this gap he was able to see along what looked like a canyon running up the face of the hill right to the top, where the sky shone brightly above the summit.

He started climbing, slowly.

It was now broad daylight, and behind the improvised walls he could hear people stirring. Halfway up the hill, quite far along one of the streets, he caught sight of a human figure – a man relieving himself into the gutter outside his front door. A famished-looking dog crept out of one of the huts, came towards him warily, sniffing, then growled when the Stranger held out a hand towards him. He suspected that any people he might meet would react likewise.

Looking back, down over the no-man's-land, into the town beyond, he saw signs of a gradual awakening. A few cars, vans, lorries were crawling about the streets. Over there, normal life was resuming.

He was curious to see what happened at the top of the hill. Did the huts swarm right over the summit, crawl down the other side? Did all the streets he had crossed continue right round, each end joining up at the back of the mountain? From the top he should be able to answer both questions.

He knew he must be only a few streets from the summit, when he made his first encounter with an adult. An elderly woman was standing outside her door, a few houses along. She beckoned to him, then put her finger to her lips in warning. She came towards him eagerly.

'Are they back yet?' she whispered.

'I don't know,' he replied.

The woman looked at him suspiciously.

'Aren't you one of them?'

The Stranger shook his head. Whoever they were, he knew he wasn't one of them.

'But you must be. An agent, surely?'

The Stranger shook his head again.

'Then what are you doing here? For you're not one of us, I know that much.'

'I . . . just came for a walk. To see.'

'To see? To see the likes of us?' The woman let out a scornful cackle which disturbed some of the other inhabitants.

Doors opened, and a few people gathered round. They stood behind the woman, listening, eyeing the Stranger suspiciously.

'Came to have a good laugh at us, did you?' went on the woman.

'I didn't come to laugh.'

'What did you come for, then? To cry, perhaps? That's all you can do with the likes of us, laugh or cry.'

A few grunts of assent from the others.

'I came to see, that's all. I came to learn. Because that's the first step.'

A wiry little man who had been standing behind some of the others now moved forward.

'You'd better go,' he said. 'There's nothing to see, there's nothing to know. Just get back to your own people, will you? Just get back.'

The Stranger bowed in silence and started walking down the steep lane again. People were stirring on either side. Some stood and stared at him, others paid no attention, secure in their numbers, on their home ground.

When he got to the bottom street he turned left to go back to the place where he had emerged from the factory area, and eventually came to the house where the little girl had crawled out. She had escaped again, and was in the middle of the narrow street, dancing gravely round and round, and humming to herself.

'*La*, la la *la* la,

La, la la *la* la . . . '

She looked up at the Stranger and gave him a mocking little smile. As if she had some mysterious source of joy, which she was wondering whether to share with him.

Just then running steps, followed by a volley of shots, were heard only a few yards away in the no-man's-land. A brawny arm emerged from the hut and the child was dragged back inside.

As the Stranger stood there, hesitating, half a dozen ragged men ran out of the opening he had been making for. One of them had blood streaming down his face. The Stranger was caught up in their frantic flight, forced to run with them in the direction he had just come from.

The wounded man staggered and fell against the Stranger, who took hold of his arm to support him as they ran.

A moment later the pursuing police rounded the corner and a hail of bullets rained on the little group.

When he recovered consciousness the Stranger tried to look about him; but he was lying on his back, and all he could see was the sky above him, and, to his left, the outline of one of the factories, while to his right he could distinguish the row of hovels that made up the first street of the Monte Pardo. He felt an intense pain in his side and gently touched the injured area. Then he looked at his hand, and saw it was covered with blood. He assumed it was his own, but then thought it might belong to the man he had been helping along when the police fired on them. His blood and my blood, he thought, and I can't tell which is which.

He tried to get up, but was too weak.

How odd, that he should be fired on by the representatives of his own class, and left to lie here, abandoned, it seemed, by both sides.

He felt neither alarm nor despair at the prospect, just surprise. Then he remembered his conviction that he had to come here, to this improbable, dreamlike mountain, and his surprise faded away. So that was it, he thought, that was why I had to come here, to lie and bleed on this soil, perhaps to die on it. Never before in his life had he felt so in tune with his surroundings. His only regret was that he hadn't actually gone to the very top of the hill, hadn't seen what it was like on the other side.

Gradually he felt he was drifting off into some form of unconsciousness – was it sleep, was it death? Blurred shapes and colours seemed to swirl about before him. Slowly a now familiar pattern emerged.

Once again he was looking at the colourful, obsessive backcloth of the Monte Pardo, rising against the sky, but now transformed, radiant; and all the doors of all the hovels were opened, and the people began coming out, streaming down the mountainside – old hags, black and twisted; young men and women, dirty and misshapen, old before their time; the halt and the lame and the deformed, limping along in the growing stream; sharp-faced children, lean and agile, darting in and out of the growing torrent of humanity; while in the foreground danced the tiny figure of the little girl, humming gravely:

'*La*, la la *la* la,
 La, la la *la* la . . . '

Living with dead miners

36

Living with dead miners

'You've changed things,' he said.

He stood in the middle of the room, turning round slowly, taking everything in.

'Where's the range? For Christ's sake, you've not done away with the range?'

'It wasn't me. The range had gone long before I bought the house.'

'Hmm! Pity, that. It was a braw range. We was all real proud of it.'

'I know. My grandmother had one. They were great things, those old ranges.'

'Old ranges!' He sounded faintly outraged. 'Ours was brand-new when we moved in. Brand-new, just like the house.'

'Of course.'

I wasn't really very sure how to tackle my visitor. He was obviously a ghost, and yet that didn't seem the right word for this man. Nothing spooky about him, apart from the fact that he'd just walked through the door – and I mean the door, not just the doorway. No, not your ordinary, ghostly sort of a ghost at all. The French word *revenant*, one who comes back, would describe him better.

From the start I knew he was a miner. After all, this was a miner's cottage I had recently moved into. And I had already got used to the presence of unseen miners crossing my garden on their way to work. How did I know they were there, if I couldn't see them? Don't ask me. I just knew.

So I wasn't altogether surprised when the phenomenon presented itself with greater definition. I could actually see this man, I could hear him, we were communicating. And I found this tremendously exciting – not so much because I was in contact with the spirit world – there really seemed very little of the spirit about my visitor – but because here was a manifestation of this vanished world of the pits that I had been so intensely aware of since coming to live in this place.

'So this is the first time you've been back? Since . . . you lived here?' I asked.

'Well, yes and no. I've been coming back regularly all along, but just outside.'

'Crossing my – I mean, the garden?'

'Yes, me and my mates. How did you know? Have you seen us?'

'No, not exactly. You know what it's like, I just sort of knew. And what made you come right in this time?'

'Same as you. I just sort of knew.'

'Knew what?'

'That it would be all right. A sort of feeling we've been getting from the house over the last few months. Reassuring.'

I too felt reassured. Since coming to live here I had

rather felt that I was an intruder, because of the persisting, unseen presence of the old community.

Now he asked:

'Seen anything of Barney?'

'Barney? Who's Barney?'

'Oh, just one of my mates. So you haven't seen him? Or heard from him?'

'No. Is there any reason why I should have come across him?'

He shrugged:

'Well, you never know. He's not an easy man to ignore, Barney isn't.'

'Noisy?' I asked.

'You could call him that. Long ago, like. We're all pretty silent these days.'

'Well, you're not, are you?'

Again he shrugged:

'Maybe not. You never know what gets through to you people.'

What did he mean with his 'you people'? The living? The outsiders who had replaced the mining community? I felt this as a setback. Either way, I was the intruder again, taking over their territory.

'Tell me about Barney. Why did you ask me about him?'

My miner was standing in the middle of the room, facing the side the range must have been in, with his hands in his trouser pockets, his shabby, shapeless jacket hanging open to reveal a once-white shirt. His battered boots were covered in coal dust, some of which had spilled over onto the carpet.

'Barney? Oh, he's a bit of a problem, is Barney.'

'In what way? What sort of a problem?'

'The thing is, we're not quite sure which side he's on.'

'Which side?'

'Well, is he still with you people, or what? Because he's never turned up – not among us, that is. And he must be nearly a hundred by now, if he's still with you lot.'

'Tell me more about him. I might be able to identify him if he's still al— . . . still with our lot.'

'He's one of those people that seems bigger than he is, like. I mean, you always know when Barney's about. Sooner or later the fur starts flying.'

'Quarrelsome, you mean?'

'Sort of. Always ready for a right barney. That's how we gave him the name.'

'So that's not his real name?'

'No. His real name's Nigel. A right sissy name for a miner.'

I agreed. But I still wanted to find out more about Barney.

'So he wouldn't be very popular, if he was always fighting?'

'Don't be daft. He was a great guy. He'd knock you out and pick you up and buy you a pint five minutes later. A real mate.'

'What did he look like?'

'Can't say, really. No distinguishing features, like they say. A miner – you could see a mile away he was one of us.'

Just then the phone rang. I went over to the window to answer it. When I turned round again he had gone.

Just a little coal dust left on the carpet, that's all.

* * *

After that all I could do to get to know more about the vanished community was keep on talking to those of my neighbours who had been here in the old days. I kept hoping the name Barney would crop up, but it never did.

And most of what I was getting was second-hand anyway, from sons and daughters of miners or even grandchildren. And they didn't seem to care much about their heritage. No nostalgia. Their conversation seldom went back further than last Christmas. They were too young, poor things, too young.

There was only one ancient man who seemed old enough to remember the glory days of the miners, and he, the old soul, was distinctly senile. He was willing to talk, bless him, but his conversation was fragmentary and disjointed.

Soon after my meeting with the ghost miner, the old man stopped for a chat while I was trimming my hedge. He was trying to tell me something about hedge-cutting, but I could make no sense of what he was saying. As the shrunken, unsteady figure tottered away, I thought what a pity that such a quiet, friendly old man should have sunk so low, both mentally and physically. He looked as if a gust of wind would blow him over.

At that moment my next-door neighbour passed.

'I see you've been having a word with the old boy. Puir auld soul, he's fair wandered.'

'A bit,' I agreed. 'He's nice, though.'

'Oh aye, he's nice enough. And harmless.'

'What's his name?'

'Oh, that's old Cameron. Barney, they used to call

him, but that's not his real name. Something a bit fancy, I think.'

'Nigel?' I suggested.

'Nigel? Yes! That's it. Who told you?'

I was still staring after the frail, unsteady figure, and didn't answer. So this was Barney – the noisy, rowdy, friendly, larger-than-life Barney. And, as I watched the diminished retreating figure, I felt the old community slipping irrevocably away.

37

Paquita's Donkey

Nobody else, but nobody, has a donkey in their front garden!

Paquita stood on the balcony outside her bedroom and looked down with a mixture of irritation and affection at the offending animal. The donkey was standing in its usual corner, motionless except for the odd twitch of an ear or the swish of its tail, as it made a token gesture to get rid of the insistent afternoon flies. Moro was an old, patient donkey, and didn't seem to worry too much about the futility of the twitching and swishing.

Paquita was young and less patient. This stupid siesta business! As if life weren't short enough anyway! But no, we have to throw away a couple of hours every day just because it's hot.

Through the open window of the room next to hers she could hear her father's quiet snoring. From the window on the other side of her room came her grandmother's regular sighing, punctuated by the occasional exclamation.

'*Ai senyor, quina calor!*'

Grandmother's feeling the heat. So am I, if it comes to that. But perhaps it's worse when you're old. Or perhaps you just make more fuss.

Again Paquita looked down at the donkey. He's old too, fifteen years older than me. That makes him thirty-five. Really quite old for a donkey. In another five years he might be dead. But in another five years I'll be old too – twenty-five, a quarter of a century, just think of it! And by then perhaps I won't mind so much about having a donkey in the front garden.

But right now I do mind. Hear that, Moro, I *mind*, I really do. Oh, I know it's not your fault, and you're a dear old thing, and I've known you all my life, but still, it's embarrassing.

She thought back to the origins of the donkey, which had been acquired as a working animal many years before Paquita had been born, when their house stood alone, a small farmhouse more than a mile from the village. At that time their village was immune from the invasion of summer visitors that flooded out of Barcelona at the beginning of every summer, escaping from the heat of the city. Cabaniu, some five miles from the coast and the railway, was considered too far from both these amenities to be of any interest to these *estiuejants*. The little farm, more than a mile inland from the village, led its quiet life year after year, with its owner, Marcel Bofill, taking his produce to the nearest town in his donkey cart every morning.

By the time the youngest granddaughter, Paquita, was born, in the early eighties, Marcel had retired. His only son, Joan, had long since found work in an office in Barcelona, and the village had grown till it had engulfed Can

Bofill, which was now doing its best to forget it had once been a *masia*, and emulate the coquettish little villas that crowded round it. For it was not the ordinary village folk who now surrounded Can Bofill, but a huge new flood of *estiuejants*, liberated by the car and the motorway from dependence on the railway.

Bit by bit, reminders of Can Bofill's farming days were eliminated. The well, for one. Who needs a well when there's piped water available from the reservoir? The outhouses had been turned into smart flats for the summer visitors. The ancient, arched doorway escaped only because one of the new villas had deliberately had a similar one put in, as a result of the recent interest in the traditional style. If people were actually building them like that, it must be chic. So the doorway remained.

And so did the donkey. The family were all fond of Moro, and, now that he too had retired, he was given a place in the part of the courtyard that had now become the front garden.

It wasn't till Paquita was eighteen that she realized the incongruity of the donkey's presence in their smart neighbourhood. She had started attending language classes in Barcelona, and was quick to notice the surprise that the donkey's presence caused her fellow students. If it hadn't been for the donkey Paquita would have managed to come to terms with the fact that she didn't live in Barcelona like most of the other students. It was a disadvantage, certainly, and she felt it placed her a few rungs down the social ladder. But still, some of the other students also lived in the surrounding villages and travelled in every day. That in itself didn't single her out as being too different. The donkey did.

Paquita rolled a sweet paper into a tight little ball and threw it at Moro. It landed on the animal's neck, and Moro gave his head a bit of a shake in acknowledgement, then settled down to his usual immobility, broken only by the inevitable twitching and swishing.

Moro! That was me, not a fly. Me, throwing a sweet paper at you. You might pay some attention. After all it's you that's my problem, the one big problem in my life. Amadeu spoke to me yesterday, you know that? Spoke to me for quite a while. And I think he might come with the others, next Sunday. Said he liked country life, and how lucky I was not to live in the city. Can't really mean it, of course. What sensible person would choose to live here, miles away from everything? I think he was just saying it because he wants to come here. And why do you think he might want to come? Eh, Moro, tell me that?

I think he likes me, Moro. I think it's *me* he likes, not country life. And it would be lovely if he came here. Only . . . Well, there's grandmother, still talking about the Civil War, as if it happened yesterday instead of more than fifty years ago. And Father still looking like a peasant, even though it's nearly thirty years since he worked the land. Well, I suppose all the others also have problems with their families. Rosa's mother looks like a tramp, even though they're so well off, and Feliu's father swears like a trooper, and Pili's brother's not quite right in the head. So I suppose it's all right to have a few discreditable people in the family.

But a donkey!

Paquita sighed with exasperation, turned back into the bedroom and lay down on the bed. Another hour to go before anyone came to life. Then she'd go and see Montsi, and they could talk about the course, for Montsi was in the same class as Paquita. About the course, and, naturally, about their fellow-students. Amadeu, for instance. Montsi had noticed her conversation with Amadeu, said something about it after they left the college. Yes, they would talk about Amadeu.

'*Ai senyor, quina calor!*' came from the neighbouring room.

For once Paquita found herself inclined to agree with her grandmother. It *was* hot. So hot that you wanted to lie down and rest; and so hot that the bed felt like a furnace, and you longed to get up again. Paquita gave a sigh of utter despair, and fell asleep.

She was roused by the sound of the television blaring vigorously in the dining room below.

Must be Grandmother. No-one else turns it on that loud. No-one else is deaf, of course. And any moment now Father will come and turn it down, and Grandmother will yell at him to turn it up again, and he'll yell back that it's too loud, that you can't even hear yourself shout in this house.

I hate falling asleep during the siesta. Feels so awful when you wake up.

She roused herself enough to get out of bed and stagger across to the balcony. She could hear the neighbours' television, rivalling their own in loudness. That one was bellowing in Castilian, their own in Catalan.

A group of ten-to-twelve-year-olds ran down the street, shouting and laughing noisily. A car drew up a few doors along, with its radio at full blast.

Paquita took in the cacophony and gave a little sigh.

That's better. Things coming alive at last. I can go and see Montsi soon, and we'll talk. About Amadeu. Other things too, of course. Don't want to give her the wrong idea. Or is it the right idea I don't want to give her? Anyway, we'll talk.

On her way out a few minutes later Paquita paused a moment beside Moro. She stood beside the donkey, patting its head with one hand, while with the other she ran a finger down the dark stripe along its back.

You're a problem, Moro. Life's difficult enough anyway. I'm not like the others in so many ways. I'm not as clever, and I still feel a bit of a country bumpkin, living out here with a family of farmers – peasants, really, that's all they were not so long ago. And my clothes are never as smart as Pili's, and my French accent will never be as good as Feliu's. And my hair's never right. It's a wonder Amadeu as much as looks at me.

And then, on top of it all – a donkey!

It was dark when she got back. Through the open window she could see her mother laying the table.

Paquita didn't feel at all like going in.

She knew exactly what it would be like. Her grandmother would scold her for not coming back earlier and helping her mother in the kitchen. Her father would tell her girls shouldn't be out alone in the dark.

But it's only nine o'clock!

Doesn't matter. It's dark, isn't it? Dark is dark, whether it's nine o'clock or midnight.

Her mother would smile her forgiving smile and ask her had she enjoyed herself? And that, of course, was the real catch. If she said yes, then she had to feel she'd been selfishly enjoying herself while her mother slaved. If she said no . . .

If she said no that would be telling the truth, and this she could not bear. Not this truth, anyway.

The girl hesitated as she stood in the doorway, then turned back to the garden, to the corner where Moro stood, a dim, motionless shape in the darkness. The flies had gone, Moro's twitching and swishing was finished for the day. The old donkey was enjoying the cool of the evening.

Paquita walked over to Moro and stood beside him, leaning against the animal's warm flank.

Oh Moro, Moro, if only you knew! A few hours ago I hated you, I really did. You are such an embarrassment, you know you are. And I couldn't bear to think it might put Amadeu off if he knew we kept a donkey – a donkey, a real donkey! that's what they all say – in the front garden. And I thought that if he said it I'd simply die of shame. And I wished you were dead, yes, I did, I really wished you were dead. Just because I couldn't bear the thought of losing him, Amadeu.

And I've lost him, Moro. Lost all hope of him, anyway, which comes to the same thing. Oh yes, I was right, he *did* want to come to Cabaniu. But it wasn't for me. It was for Montsi. He's in love with Montsi – he's actually told her – and she's in love with him. And I'm in love with him too. Only I'll never be able to tell him.

At least I didn't give anything away. I didn't let her guess, I'm sure I didn't.

All those hours sitting there chatting with Montsi, with her family, with other friends, waiting till the usual time to come home, holding back the tears.

Paquita leaned closer against the donkey. She put both arms round its shoulders and, slumping down against the animal, let her head rest on its neck. After a while her tears began to form a little channel down the coarse hairs along Moro's neck.

Moro stood perfectly still, his head down. Once only, when he felt the girl's tears trickling down his neck, he twitched his ears. Then he returned to his usual night-time immobility. Like a rock.

38

38

Dark Journey

A darkened, almost black, landscape, with a train crossing it. A caterpillar of light boring its way through the
darkness. Sometimes it moves slowly, so slowly that you
can make out the individual windows, with the people
sitting behind them. Sometimes it pierces the darkness
at such speed that all you can see is the streak of light,
and the imagination has to fill in the windows with the
passengers sitting behind them.

Sometimes the landscape the train crosses is a flat,
endlessly flat, plain. You can only just make out the
geometrical pattern of fields, one after another, receding
into infinity. One field, and then another, and then another.
And beyond and behind, more fields and yet more fields.
An infinite extension of dark, flat fields, with hardly a tree
to break the monotony. And travelling through this infinity
is the train, the shining jewel – light and sharpness and
motion, against the unending, unmoving, parcelled-out
darkness.

Sometimes the landscape is flat but empty – no half-
seen chessboard here. No fields, no trees, no hedges,

walls or fences, just the unending, everlasting steppe. Black emptiness pierced by the shining insect crawling across it, so far away in this immensity that the windows run together to make one continuous streak of light.

And then at times the landscape becomes active, joins in the game. A hill or a mountain rises up, and the train disappears behind a mass of rock, or vanishes inside a tunnel. When it reappears it may run beside a river, and two shining creatures race along, keeping exact pace with each other, unfailingly together. You can never tell which is the train and which the reflection.

The one thing that all these different versions of the train have in common is that it never arrives at its destination. It never stops.

You make up stories about the passengers, you know many of them by sight, you look out for your favourites. They're always there. You are sure of that; even when the train is going so fast that you can't make out the individual windows, much less the passengers, you feel their familiar presence. The old man with the pince-nez and the mildly astonished expression, the fat girl with the happy smile, the woman who looks like a retired film star, the middle-aged housewife surrounded by her host of parcels, the young man with thinning hair and a passion for crosswords, the thirty-something couple who seldom have anything to say to each other, the young man with a shock of red hair . . . Oh, and the dark, pretty girl who always has a book to read but who spends most of the time staring out of the window into the darkness.

No children. There are never any children on the train. But then, you're not interested in children.

* * *

There's a conversation going on between the retired film star and the young man doing crosswords.

'You do a lot of crosswords?' she asks.

'Oh yes, I love them. Do you?'

'I used to be good at them. Are you stuck with any of the clues?'

'There's this one: "Calcium begins and ends this dance round its capital." Seven letters. It should be easy, for the calcium bit must be Ca.'

'Why must it be Ca?'

'Because that's the symbol for calcium.'

'In that case it's *carioca*.'

'Is that a dance?'

'Of course it's a dance! Brazilian. And the capital's Rio.'

'But it isn't', says the young man. 'The capital of Brazil is Brasilia.'

'Then your crossword's got it wrong. Lots of people make that mistake. Everybody's heard of Rio and no-one's heard of Brasilia.'

'But crosswords don't get things wrong.' There's a tremor of anxiety in the young man's voice.

'This one has. It simply has to be *carioca*. It all fits in perfectly.' The ex-star looks critically at the young man. She thinks she can see why his hair is thinning.

'You worry too much,' she says. 'What does it matter if the crossword's got it wrong for once?'

'No, but it hasn't. It mustn't, it can't,' the man pleads.

Outside, the blackness rolls past them endlessly. The young man with the thinning hair looks from the fading

126

glamour of his companion to the blackness outside, then back to the woman. He feels as if a little of the darkness has seeped into the carriage.

The old man with the pince-nez and the fat girl have got talking.

'It's a long journey, in the dark,' says the old man.

'I know. Feels like we're never going to get there.' She smiles brightly all the same.

'Yes. It feels as if we were never going to get there,' corrects the man.

The girl doesn't notice. 'Haven't seen my boyfriend for three months,' she volunteers cheerfully. 'We're meeting at the airport tomorrow.'

'Have you been away somewhere?'

'No, he has. Been in Abu Dhabi. Working.'

'I suppose we've all been away, in a manner of speaking.'

'*I* haven't.'

'We all have,' the man insists. 'Some of us don't notice.'

'*I* would notice if I was away. And I'm not, and I wasn't.'

'You mean you've never been away, ever, anywhere?'

'Course I have! But not now. Not while my boyfriend's been in Abu Dhabi.'

'And yet that would have been a good time to be away.'

'I know. With him. But he wouldn't let me. Said it was no place for a woman. I suppose he knew what he was talking about. He'd been there before.'

'Do you think most of us know what we're talking about?'

'*I* do. Don't know about you.'

'No, I don't either.' The man's expression has become increasingly astonished. 'I mean, it's all so utterly unaccountable, isn't it?'

'What is?'

'Everything. That's what makes it so fascinating. You never know, do you? You never, never know.'

'Never know what?'

'Anything. All this darkness outside,' and he points towards the solid black behind the window, 'and is it any better in here?'

The girl looks at him in surprise, and gradually the confident smile fades from her face. She turns to the window and looks out, trying to pierce the blackness. Then she looks along the carriage, puzzled. Have the lights dimmed a little, or is she just imagining it?

The housewife hasn't managed to start a conversation with the married couple so far. She keeps looking expectantly at them as they sit opposite her. If only one of them would speak to the other, that might give her an opening. But, for a long time, they seem to have nothing to say.

At last the man speaks:

'Never came, did they?'

'No, they didn't.'

The man grunts, then adds, 'Just like them.'

The housewife sighs, unable to consider the conversation sufficiently general to warrant an intervention.

She looks at the parcels on the seat beside her, seeking inspiration. New dress, bath sponge, three pairs of tights, set of table mats, lampshade for the sitting room, gardening gloves, spatula for the kitchen, pair of slippers – not that she needed them, they just looked nice. Try as she will, she simply can't find suitable material in that lot for a convincing opening gambit.

A question, she thinks, that's always admissible. But what question? That is the question, she thinks, as number one of her small stock of Shakespeare quotations rises to the surface. This strikes her as comical, and she has to convert a giggle into a cough.

The peculiar sound prompts the man to look at her.

Seizing her chance, she blurts out the first words that come into her mind:

'Do you think we'll get there in time?'

'In time for what?' asks the man.

'Oh, nothing in particular. Just in time.'

'If it's *in* time, it must be in time *for* something. What you mean is *on* time.'

'Do I?' The woman is aware that she didn't really mean anything at all. She just wanted to start a conversation.

The wife throws her husband a reproachful look:

'You're very rude, Robert. You can't go about telling people what they mean.' Turning to the housewife:

'He's like that, you know. Always putting people right, always got to be right. He's a teacher.'

'Which explains everything,' remarks the man in a tone of heavy irony.

The housewife wonders whether to resent the man's manner or continue the conversation, since she now has something she cannot fail to consider as an opening. She opts for the latter course.

'And what do you teach?' she asks brightly.

'Mostly morons.'

The housewife recognizes this as an authentic convers-
ation-stopper, and subsides into silence.

By way of apology for her husband's rudeness, the
wife takes up the conversational cudgels.

'Been shopping?' she asks.

The housewife's face lights up. 'Yes, I've had a really
busy day. Such a lot of odds and ends I needed, and
I've really only got half of them. Terrible the number of
things we need, isn't it?'

'Terrible the number of things we *think* we need. Some
of us, at least.'

'Oh, Herbert, you're being rude again. I'm sure this
lady's not been buying anything she doesn't need.'

'Well, there *were* the slippers . . . '

The wife smiles reassuringly. 'Oh, but that's nothing.
A pair of slippers are nothing.'

'A pair of slippers *is* nothing,' corrects her husband.

'Well, what's the difference?' asks his wife.

'No difference, no difference at all. Just like long and
short, or good and bad, or black and white, or darkness
and day.' The man glares at his wife and their companion. 'Just you look out there!' And he points to the window. 'What do you see there, eh? Trees and fields and
perhaps the odd ruminating cow? What's that you said?
You can't see a thing? Because it's dark, you say? And
yet you can't tell the difference, so how do you know it's
dark, eh? Just tell me, how do you know?'

'I never said I couldn't tell the difference between
darkness and day. Did I, now?' The woman appeals to the
housewife, who, feeling rather uneasy, mutters something
indistinct.

'Can't tell the difference between singular and plural,'

pursues the man. 'Can't tell the difference between darkness and day. Same thing, absolutely the same thing. But I can tell. I can tell it's pitch-black out there. Pitch-black.' He glares angrily from his wife to their companion.

Cowed, the housewife repeats his words. '*Pitch*-black,' she assents. And a little shiver runs through her.

'Is it very dull?' asks the young man with the red hair.

'Is what very dull?' The pretty girl looks up, as if she'd just been dragged back from somewhere miles away.

'Your book. You've not read a single word for at least twenty minutes. Just sat there looking out into the darkness. As if there was anything to see!'

'But there is, there's plenty to see.'

'Out there? It's dark outside, hadn't you noticed?'

'I'm not looking outside, I'm looking inside.'

'And what do you see inside?'

'Dreams. Just . . . dreams.'

'Nice ones?'

'Some of them.'

'Don't suppose I'm in any of them – am I?'

'Why should you be?'

'Because I'm here, and I'm real. Much more real than your dreams.'

'I'm not so sure about that.'

'About the fact that I'm more real than your dreams? Oh, come on! The very definition of "dream" implies unreality.'

'Reality's not that important,' says the girl dismissively. She hopes the intrusive young man will realize he's been politely snubbed.

He does. After a moment he gets up and moves along

the carriage, while the girl plunges her liberated gaze deep into the creative blackness outside.

The ex-star sees the red-haired young man walking along the corridor, looking rather aimless. She has seen, though not heard, his conversation with the pretty girl. She gives him a welcoming smile.

'Are you good at crosswords?' she asks.

He smiles back gratefully and sits down.

'Not really. Well, sometimes. Are you stuck on something?' he asks the young man with thinning hair.

'Yes. Neither of us can get this one. "In the end I lie on top of a cubic centimetre to get this series." Nine letters. The cubic centimetre must be CC, and we've already got a C near the end – third last letter – so this confirms it. And the fourth letter seems to be O. Any ideas?'

Redhead looks at Thinning Hair, then shakes his head. He looks out into the darkness rushing past, and feels it's not his day. Or rather, it's not his night, for it seems to have been dark for a very long time.

The husband, tired of glaring at his wife and their companion, gets up and saunters along the carriage to the little group engaged in the crossword.

'Read that clue again,' he commands.

Obediently, Thinning Hair repeats it.

'Fibonacci,' states the husband. 'Never heard of the Fibonacci series?' Faced with three blank faces he tut-tuts loudly and turns away.

The ex-star puts out a hand to stop him:

'How do you spell it?'

The husband looks at the elegantly groomed hand resting on his arm and spells the word out.

'Thank you so much.' The hand administers a grateful little pat to the arm. The arm begins to move away again, then its owner changes his mind and sits down. 'Let's see now,' he says, reaching out for the paper.

Meekly, Thinning Hair hands it over, while the husband takes a pen out of his breast pocket. It's evident he means business.

Redhead feels ousted once again and wanders a little further along the carriage to where the fat girl and the old man with the pince-nez are gazing out at the darkened, almost invisible landscape – the girl looking disconsolate, the man gently amazed.

'It's a long journey,' announces Redhead as he sits down.

The girl looks at him, enraptured.

'It is, isn't it? I was just saying, like we're never going to get there.'

'Right,' says Redhead, relieved. He seems to have struck the right note at last.

He and the girl chat happily, on and on, about her boyfriend, her plans and hopes, Redhead's plans and hopes, the weather, the time, the latest films and pop tunes. The old man watches them, the astonishment in his gaze tempered by a gentle, nostalgic approval. Once or twice he adjusts his pince-nez and gazes at the couple more closely, then scrutinizes the darkness outside. He shakes his head, as if he can't reconcile the two pictures.

Left to themselves, the wife and the housewife start a serious conversation on the subject of *husbands*. Their agreement is total. Within a few minutes they feel like sisters and have forgotten all about the train and the darkness outside.

'Now, *mine*', says the housewife, 'is the most generous of men. That I have to admit. All this,' she waves at her purchases, 'he'll never ask how much I spent, or what I got. He gives me everything but his attention. And that's the trouble, you see. He just doesn't care what I buy. Never even looks to see what I'm wearing.'

'Now, *mine* . . . '

And they carry on happily, catching up on lost time, racing along, knowing that at last they're getting somewhere. It may be dark outside, but they are too engrossed in their own small illumination to notice.

The dark, pretty girl sits by herself, gazing out. As the train slows to take a curve in the line she sees the first carriage come into view – a series of illuminated windows, radiant, orderly; a moving chain of light, enhanced by and yet denying the velvety darkness it pierces but cannot dispel.

39

And two windows

'Go away! Go away!'

The American tourist waved an arm in a sort of shooing gesture, to make his meaning clearer to this small but persistent beggar. The child darted under the outstretched arm, behind the two massive bodies, and appeared at the side of the woman, with his hand held out as before. Barely looking at him, the woman dropped a few coins into the small hand.

'You shouldn't, Elna. You know you shouldn't. It only encourages them.'

'Well, I dunno. It also gets rid of them.'

Peret didn't wait to hear the conversation. He could have told you exactly how it would go. You didn't need to speak English to understand the dynamics of the thing. Sometimes it was the wife who relented, sometimes the husband. Some days it was neither. And today had been, on the whole, one of the empty days.

The sun was beginning to dip down behind the higher buildings of the centre of the city. It was time to start the long walk back to the shantytown where he lived.

But pickings had been poor today and he was afraid to go back virtually empty-handed. Paco would make a fuss, yell at him, probably beat him.

Ahead of him he saw a coachload of tourists setting off to discover the city. They were going in the wrong direction for Peret, but he decided he'd better follow them. Surely one of them at least would give him something? It took him quite a while to get through the coachload, for they split up into two groups, each taking a different direction. By the time he'd finished with the first group he'd lost sight of the second, but he'd seen which way they had gone, and ran to catch up with them.

This lot seemed a bit different from the average tourist. Instead of wandering about, stopping, starting, taking everything in, they moved quickly and purposefully along, with a leader at their head. It was hard work keeping up with them. Most of them paid little attention to the skinny little boy running along beside them with his hand outstretched and a pitiful expression on his thin face. But those who actually looked at him were struck by the waif-like appearance of the child. The face was dominated by the two great dark eyes under a wide forehead. The rest of the face, with its receding chin, seemed to melt away into a scrawny neck above a thin, wiry body. He looked rather like an anxious and highly mobile tadpole, swept along by the current of tourists.

Just as Peret was about to approach the last of the tourists, the whole party turned into a large official-looking building, and he was left standing by himself on the pavement. He now realized for the first time that he was in a completely unknown part of the town.

Streetwise as he was, he felt a little quiver of fear rising in him. He had spent his life on the streets of this city, but he only knew the very centre, with its wealth of tourists. From where he was now he had no idea how to get on to the road that would take him back to the huge shantytown on the outskirts. He tried to find his way back to where he had joined the tourists in the centre of the town; but the column of visitors had snaked their way along a number of back streets, and he soon lost all track of the way they had come.

He was tired, and sat down on the pavement to count the coins in his pocket. Not too bad. Perhaps he would escape a beating after all. He leaned against the wall and indulged in one of his favourite fantasies. He was back in the hovel with Paco and the other boys. And a beating was going on. Only, this time it was Peret who was in charge. He was grasping the broken chair leg that was usually used for the purpose, and he was beating a subdued and powerless Paco, to the great delight of the other boys, all of whom were familiar with the feel of the instrument.

Soon his daydream melted away, and a wave of panic swept over him. How would he ever find his way back?

He began running at random, dodging in and out of the people on the pavement. If he didn't get back soon Paco would beat him for being late. The further he ran, the more unfamiliar the streets became. In the end despair took over and he began to cry.

Still he kept on running, blinded by tears, bumping into people, bouncing off them, tripping over feet . . .

And then he felt a strong hand gripping him by the shoulder, and giving him a good shake into the bargain.

'Let me go! Let me go!' the boy squealed, trying to wriggle free.

* * *

Manel was in a filthy temper. One of those days when everything had gone wrong. A cold wind, poor pickings, a brush with the police . . . Normally he took these little upsets in his stride, reminding himself that this was how things were. But today every little annoyance had somehow got under his skin. The real problem, of course, was tomorrow.

Tomorrow meant the start of a new job, always a stressful experience. And life had taught him that new jobs never seemed to get much beyond that stage. They always ceased to be jobs before they stopped being new. Either he was sacked for incompetence, driven out by his mates for not pulling his weight, or else he simply walked out, unable to stand the boredom of doing the same repetitive job in the same dull place day after day . . . For who wants to spend the greater part of every day sweeping the streets or carrying bales of cotton or unloading bricks from an eternal line of lorries? Whatever the reason, he was bound to be out of a job again within days, or at most a week or two.

He was making his way through the busy streets, crowded with evening workers heading for home, when he felt a kick on his shin, and nearly fell over the small figure that had run into him. Grabbing a meagre shoulder, he gave it a violent shake, and held its terrified owner at arm's length.

'What the hell d'you think you're doing, running into people like that? Can't you look where you're going?'

Two startled big eyes were gazing up at him. A skinny hand had come up, ready to ward off the expected blow.

And Manel, who had been on the point of striking, paused with raised hand. Something in the child's attitude had reminded him of the little boy he had been not so many years ago, squirming to get free from his violent father.

With an angry shake, he threw the boy aside and walked on. His childhood was something he preferred to forget. Beatings, hunger, rags, and an atmosphere of constant uncertainty, frequently turning to fear. His already sombre mood darkened even further at this reminder of the black cloud that had hung over his early years. The present was bad enough, without being reminded of earlier and even greater miseries. La Piedad, for instance.

Peret staggered backwards and ended up sprawled against a wall. The main emotion he felt was surprise. Why had the man not hit him? After all, there was nothing to stop him. Peret was not used to being spared in this way. After a moment's astonishment he came to a hasty decision, and started to run after Manel, whom he now began to think of as a possible benefactor. For who else would have let him off with nothing but a shove and a shake?

Certainly not Paco, anyway.

For a while Manel strode gloomily on, with Peret trotting along at his heels. The child was trying to find out as much as he could about his prospective new master. He noticed the shabby clothes – torn jeans and a faded tee-shirt, none too clean. And Manel's body language was far from reassuring. It was clear he wasn't in the best of tempers. But then, if you compared him with Paco . . . And Peret gave a soft whistle, to indicate the astronomical difference between the two men. For Paco looked as if he would kick rather than walk, and his hands were always at the ready to shower blows on more or less anyone who came within his reach. And no urchin that ran into him would escape a few heavy blows at the very least.

They came to a halt at a set of traffic lights. As they waited Manel became aware of the small figure beside him, and wondered vaguely if this could be the boy who had run into him. But his mind was too taken up with the impending misery of the next day, and by the time the lights had changed he had forgotten all about the youngster.

The same thing happened at the next traffic lights. This time Manel happened to look down just as Peret was looking up at him, and he recognized the big dark eyes with their frightened expression.

'You following me?' He didn't know whether to be annoyed or amused.

Peret nodded.

'Why?'

'Because you didn't hit me.'

Manel laughed. 'But there are dozens of other people about and they didn't hit you. Why don't you follow them?'

'But I didn't kick them, so why should they hit me?'

'And why did you kick me?' Just then Manel saw that the lights had changed. 'Come on!' Once again he grabbed the boy by the shoulder, this time to drag him across the street.

'But I didn't mean to kick you! It was just that I got frightened and I was running about, trying to find my way back . . . '

'Back to where?'

'Back to Paco. Because he always beats me if I'm late.'

'And who's Paco?'

'My protector.'

Manel burst out laughing.

Peret didn't see the joke.

'It's not all that funny, having a protector. I wish I'd a father instead.'

'A father? A father can beat you too.'

'That's different. A father has a right to beat you. But he'll look after you too. A protector doesn't.'

Manel was about to point out that some fathers didn't look after you either, but instead he asked:

'Where do you live, then?'

'In La Piedad.'

'That's a pretty rough quarter, isn't it?'

Peret shrugged. 'I didn't choose to live there, did I? I'd rather live here, in one of these nice houses, with proper doors and windows. Is this where you live?' And Peret looked with admiration at the neat rows of prosperous buildings on either side of the street.

'Not likely. But I do have a door and two windows, so I suppose—'

'*Two* windows?'

Manel reflected that it was for the sake of that one door and two windows that he was starting work tomorrow. After a longish spell living on his luck, which sometimes let him down, he'd been warned by the landlord that he'd be out in the street if some rent wasn't forthcoming soon. And that, he had decided, was worse than anything. Worse even than work. No, whatever happened, he wasn't going to run the risk of being homeless again.

Meanwhile, what was he going to do with this youngster?

'Don't you think it's time you got back to La Piedad?'

'I don't know how to get there. I was lost before I met you, and now I'm more lost than ever.'

'It's on the other side of the town. You've got to go right through the centre again.'

'But that's where I got lost.'

This was not strictly true; but the appeal of the one door and two windows seemed to justify the slight inaccuracy.

Life had taught Peret how to size people up as far as social standing goes. It was clear that this young man was far from rich; but still, a door and two windows seemed to indicate something a bit better than the shantytown he had spent all his life in. He'd have given anything to see the place, and perhaps, even . . . After all, this man was the friendliest adult he'd come across in years.

'Then you'll just have to ask someone the way.'

The boy shook his head. 'It doesn't work that way. Not when you're eight years old, not when you're dressed in rags. They think you're just begging and so they chase you off; or they might just throw a coin at you. Or else they think you're trying to pick their pocket and—'

'And are you trying to pick their pocket?'

'Yes, of course. Sometimes, anyway. What else can I do? Paco beats me if I don't bring back enough, and you never get that much from begging, do you?'

'You can say that again!'

Once again Manel was reliving his youth. It had taken him till he was twelve to find the courage to run away from his father and fend for himself – stealing and begging at first, then finding work to tide him over for a spell. Then more stealing, whenever he walked out of a job or was thrown out. But he'd given up the begging. A man has to have some standards.

They had stopped at a crossroads. The centre of the town had been left well behind and they were in what had once been a village, but had now been swallowed up by the city. Small shops, factories, warehouses, blocks of tawdry flats and decrepit little one-storey houses were all jumbled together.

For a moment the young man and the boy stared at each other in silence. Manel was having a battle with himself. For the last seven years he had valued his independence more than anything else. On the other hand, here was this kid, with his big pleading eyes and his undernourished body . . .

'Come on! I'll show you my place.'

He told himself he was only doing this because the boy had amused him, and taken his mind off tomorrow and work. But when he saw the sparkle in the boy's eyes he felt glad he'd done something to lighten the sadness in them.

Manel's place consisted of one room in an ancient, shabby house deep in a warren of tumbledown buildings. He led the boy through a twisting corridor, past several half-open doors from which the acrid smell of food frying in cheap oil floated out, and came to a door at the back of the house. Manel opened it with proprietorial pride and revealed a small, rather bare room with two windows giving on to a courtyard with a water pump in the middle.

'Well, this is it.'

Peret stepped in almost reverently and made straight for one of the windows.

'Shutters, too,' he murmured. Then turning round to inspect the room itself he almost whispered:

'And a table and two chairs – and a bed! You live like a prince!'

Manel laughed.

'And I've even got some food in the house.'

He opened a corner cupboard and took out some provisions – a loaf of coarse bread, three sardines, some olives.

'Sit down,' he said.

That night Manel lay awake a long time, his mind busy with memories of his earlier years.

La Piedad! The name still had the power to bring a chill to his thoughts.

Manel had made for this place when he first left home, and had spent a short time there, in much the same situation as Peret's. His 'protector' had been as violent as his father, so his lot was hardly improved. But it had the advantage of not being binding; and after a few weeks he had decided he'd be better on his own, sleeping rough in the city centre, living from hand to mouth, but independent.

Since then he had had a real horror of the place, and had sworn nothing would ever tempt him again into La Piedad. The name still evoked a vision of want, disorder, foul smells, quarrels, and the weird, pitiful howling of the idiot girl next door suddenly breaking the silence of the night.

Next morning Peret woke up much later than usual. No-one had given him the usual clout or kick. He opened his eyes and awareness came flooding back. He really was in a proper room, with a door and windows. He really was lying on a comfortable heap of old clothes in one of the corners. And his friend had gone off, as expected.

'I'll have to go off early, I've got this job. But I'll be back in the evening. Just you stay here till I come back,' Manel had said.

Peret lay still, enjoying his leisure, feeling secure and at ease. He could hardly believe his good fortune. Nothing had been said about a permanent arrangement, but he had a feeling this was how things would work out.

He kept on examining every detail of the room, comparing it with the series of ramshackle huts that constituted Paco's abode. Here the walls were properly built, plastered and whitewashed; there, the walls were made up of odd sheets of plastic or corrugated metal, with a few pieces of cardboard to fill in the gaps. Here the door was made of wood, and had a handle; there an old shawl or blanket was all you could hope for, and was liable to be pinched at any time by someone whose own door substitute had been blown away, or stolen in its turn.

He thought with satisfaction of how annoyed Paco would be at his defection. Not that his protector would make any serious attempt at tracking him down. His was a rather fluid establishment. People came and people went, and no questions were asked. And Peret knew only too well that his daily contribution was often so small as to make Paco threaten to throw him out. He might well have been better on his own; but he was always deterred by the memory of the hunger and want he had suffered a few years earlier when his mother had abandoned him to go off with a man who refused to take the child too. At that time even Paco, with his harsh treatment and scanty rewards, had seemed an improvement on having to fend for himself.

After a while of meditating on his altered circumstances he got up and went out into the courtyard where the latrines were. He had just got back into the room and was about to close the door when a big man came running along the corridor, charged into the room, grabbed Peret by the scruff of the neck, and began shaking him vigorously.

'Got you, my lad! Thought you'd get away with it, did you? Thought nobody'd notice, eh? Well, I notice, I know what's going on, I do. Got eyes in the back of my head, I have. Need them, in a town like this, with vermin like you about.'

Every sentence was punctuated by another ferocious shake.

'And I won't have thieves on my property, get that? I won't have thieves!'

Peret was trying to explain, but at first he simply couldn't get through to the irate owner of the property. In the end he managed to make himself heard:

'But he said I was to wait here till he got back in the evening. He told me to wait.'

'He? He? Who's he, might I ask?'

'The . . . the man who lives here.'

'Well, what's his name?'

Peret shook his head in dismay. He hadn't thought of asking his friend's name.

'You don't know, is that it? You don't even know what he's called. And you expect me to believe he wants you here, prowling about his room?'

'I was not prowling! He said—'

But by this time the man had dragged Peret along the corridor and to the front door, shaking and kicking him as he went.

'Here! This is the place for you, the street. That's where you belong,' he said as he gave the boy an even more ferocious parting kick. 'Don't let me see you skulking around here ever again. Next time I'll break every bone in your body, I will.'

With that he flung the child right across the street. Peret ended up in a crumpled heap on the opposite pavement.

'Caught him stealing in my house,' explained the man to a woman who was passing with a loaded shopping basket. 'They're up to all sorts, they are, these brats.'

'Scum!' agreed the woman. 'They're all over the place. I don't know why they don't lock them all up.'

Peret lay on the pavement, too dazed to even try to get up. But, looking across, he saw the man was still standing in the doorway, watching him. Bruised and battered as he was, he felt he'd better get out of the man's sight, and dragging himself up, he hobbled round the next few corners. He came to an old, disused stable with some rotting straw on the floor. After looking round to see there was no-one about to chase him off, he limped over to the darkest corner and lay down.

Manel had found the day less trying than he expected. His job was to sweep up the scraps from the cuttings in a large clothes factory, to run errands and carry bundles of clothes at different stages of completion from one department to another. Not too tiring, and more varied than most of the other soulless employments he had tried so far. And all the time he was thinking of the boy who would be waiting for him at home. He had enjoyed the child's awed admiration of his modest dwelling. It had raised his own self-esteem and made him realize that for the last few years he had paid for his independence with loneliness. And there was something else. For the first time in his life he had been able to offer hospitality to another human being. This thought brought him an increase in confidence. He now began to see himself as a member of society, not as an outcast.

On the way back he stopped at a small, overcrowded grocer's shop and bought some food – more bread, tomatoes, some cold meat, some fruit . . . Peret would no doubt call this a feast, he decided, and smiled at the thought of the boy's enjoyment.

'I'm back,' he announced as he opened the door.

The room was empty.

Later, as he recalled that moment, he was surprised at the intensity of the disappointment he had felt. Disappointment that ultimately turned to disquiet as he paced about the room waiting for Peret to return.

After a while he went out into the courtyard and spoke to a man who was filling his pail at the pump.

'Benito, have you seen anything of a boy hanging about here?'

'What sort of a boy? How old?'

'About eight, I think he said.'

'Oh, that'll be the boy Blas chased out this morning. He caught him stealing in your room.'

'Stealing? He wasn't stealing! I told him to wait there till I got back. And anyway, there's nothing worth stealing in my room.'

'Nor in mine neither. Not one of us has anything to steal, except for Blas. That's why he's always on the lookout for thieves.'

But Manel wasn't listening any longer. He had set off to look for the landlord. When he found him the two of them had a blazing row, with Manel complaining that Blas had no right to throw out his guest, and Blas maintaining that he would throw out whoever he pleased, and would start on Manel himself if he didn't shut up. And if he ever saw that urchin again he would break every bone in his body, he would.

'That's what I told him, so you won't be seeing him here again, for I gave him a good taste of what he'll get next time I catch him skulking about.'

Manel felt a fierce desire to take his landlord by the throat and throttle him. Instead he stormed out of the house and began wandering up and down all over the neighbourhood, hoping against hope he would come across Peret. At one point he passed by the very stable where the boy was still lying. He looked in, but saw only what he took to be a heap of old clothes; and Peret, who had fallen into a troubled sleep, didn't see the figure in the doorway.

Manel turned away, walked a bit further, came back to his room in the hope that Peret had come back, then wandered off again. He didn't know what to do. Should he cross the town and try La Piedad, just in case the boy had gone back to his old home? But La Piedad was a long way off and he was afraid to stay away from his room for too long. What if the boy came back when he was away?

He'll come back, he's bound to come back, he kept telling himself. And then he remembered what sort of threats Blas had flung at the boy, and his hopes sank again. Assuming Peret actually had the courage to come back, he might be in real danger. Manel knew only too well how violent Blas could be.

He was pacing about the courtyard when old Ramona came up to him.

'What's got into you?' she said. 'Been coming and going and going and coming all evening like an agitated hen. Can't you sit still?'

'No, I can't. I'm worried about that boy.'

'What boy?'

'The one Blas threw out this morning.'

'Oh yes, I heard about that. Did he steal anything from you?'

'No, he didn't. He wasn't here to steal. He'd a perfect right to be here. And that bloody Blas threw him out. And he's probably hurt and wandering about homeless, and . . . and I feel responsible.'

He explained how he had met Peret and brought him back with him. 'So, you see, it's all my fault. Only, I don't know what I did wrong.'

'I'll tell you what you did wrong. You should have told Blas about it. You know what he's like – wants to be in control of everything all the time. And pretty violent when he's crossed.'

Manel sighed. 'And I thought I was doing the right thing by the boy, and it's all turned out wrong.'

'Well, don't just stand there lamenting. If you take responsibility for another human being you've got to learn the rules. Other people exist too, you know – even the ones you don't like. Even landlords. You've got to take them into account just the same. So you'll simply have to go and explain the whole thing to Blas. After all, he's the boss here. We've all got to do as he wishes. – yes, eat humble pie, that's what you've got to do. For if you don't, and the boy comes back, he'll give him an even worse thrashing.'

Manel was standing still, thinking about this idea of taking responsibility for someone else. He hadn't realized this was what he was doing last night when he asked the boy in and shared his meal with him. As for the rules that Ramona had spoken about . . . Yes, he saw it now; if he'd only told Blas about the boy, none of this would have happened.

'I suppose,' he said, 'I suppose I'd better go and see Blas, just in case the boy comes back.' But this wasn't his only reason for seeing Blas. Ramona's words had made him realize for the first time that people were interconnected, that what you did had consequences for other people; that you couldn't just ignore them and get away with it.

He knocked on Blas's door, feeling apprehensive and yet at the same time more grown up than he had ever felt before. He was behaving the way proper grown-ups behave.

A scowling Blas stood before him. 'Well, what is it now?'

'I . . . I think there's been a bit of a misunderstanding. About that boy, I mean.'

No sound from Blas.

'I mean, I realize now, perhaps I should have told you about him when I went out in the morning.'

'Well, why didn't you? Eh? Why didn't you?'

'I just didn't think of it. I was starting a new job and well . . . You know how it is.'

'Do I?' Blas was evidently not going to make it easy for his young tenant.

Manel was tempted to walk away, but the thought of the danger this might mean for Peret won the day.

'I'm sorry, señor Blas. I'm really very sorry.'

Blas allowed his scowl to relax and announced that the apology was accepted.

'And, if the boy comes back, you won't . . . ?'

Blas shook his head solemnly. 'I won't.'

Manel spent the rest of the evening wandering about, looking for his lost protégé. Every time he saw a small figure in the distance, his heart gave a leap. Could it be Peret?

In the end he decided he'd better go to La Piedad. After all, where else could the child be? Knowing how Blas had treated the boy, and how he had threatened him, he realized it would take sheer heroism on Peret's part to go near the room with two windows that had so impressed him.

It was a long walk, right through the centre of the town, past a dreary no-man's-land, half town, half country; then came the first of the hovels of the huge shantytown.

It was dark by the time he got there. The uneven rows of ill-lit, tumble-down dwellings seemed even more sordid and sinister than he remembered them. There were few people about in the streets, but inside the huts could be seen shadowy forms moving about, or sitting in the doorway. The place seemed strangely silent, as if all these half-seen forms were waiting, listening, watching.

Manel felt ill at ease, threatened by the implicit violence of this huge, flimsy city.

Seven years, he thought. Seven years, and nothing has changed. These people are every bit as poor as they were, living off the spoils and the waste from the city. I see why Peret was so impressed by my door and windows. A proper door here must be a real luxury.

Now and then a furtive figure would scurry out of one of the hovels and disappear into the darkness. Manel saw no-one that could possibly be Peret.

Besides, this place was so huge that even if the boy was wandering about these streets, if that's what you could call this disorderly collection of alleys, the chances of running into him were minimal.

In the distance a weird, unearthly howling started. With a shiver of dread Manel recognized the voice of the idiot girl who used to live next door. It seemed wrong, impossible that something that he had left so far behind should still be going on the same as before. She must be grown up by now, he thought, and yet nothing has changed for her. It's as if a curse had been laid on all these poor people, as if they had been for ever condemned to a world of want and misery and crime, where time stands still.

Rounding a corner, he stumbled into a can of rubbish, which fell over with a clatter. At once several dogs started barking, a child began to cry, and a number of dark shadows emerged from the nearest huts. In an instant Manel was surrounded by a circle of swirling dogs and cursing men.

He was trying to explain what he was there for when a strident female voice cut through the general uproar and an old, bent woman pushed her way to the front of the group. In the dim light emerging from the nearest hut

Manel recognized La Serpiente, the most powerful inhab-
itant of the shantytown. Known as the Serpent because of
the venom she continually spat forth, she had been a figure of terror to the young Manel; and even now, grown
up as he was, he felt the familiar dread and apprehension
that the sight of her and the sound of her had invariably
aroused in him.

She picked out the stranger who was the cause of the
uproar, and planted herself squarely in front of him.

'Back inside, you lot,' she ordered the others. 'I'll deal
with this customer. So,' she said as the men sulked back
to their hovels, 'what are you doing here, disturbing these
good, law-abiding people at this time of night? *Eh?*' She
spat the syllable out.

'I'm looking for a boy.'

'A boy, is it? A boy? Plenty of boys here – if you're
prepared to pay for them. Ha, ha! We'll fit you out with
a boy all right, if that's what you're looking for.'

'No, it's not that.' Manel was too frightened to show
the anger he felt. 'It's a boy called Peret I'm looking
for.'

'Peret? That miserable little runt! More like a tadpole
than a boy. He'll grow into a frog, that one will, if he
lives that long. You could do better than Peret.'

'No, it's not that. I just want to talk to Peret.'

The old woman gave a short, cackling laugh.

'Well, there's no accounting for tastes. You'll have to
see Paco about that. Paco!' she bellowed in a surprisingly
powerful voice.

A distant yell followed in reply, and a moment later
a thick-set, middle-aged man with a bald head and huge
side-whiskers appeared. Manel recognized him as one of

the most brutal bullies in the place – a man who was constantly in trouble with the police. He seemed to be just as given to breaking the law as the others were, but rather less intelligent and more vicious. On one occasion he had been suspected of beating one of his charges to death. Manel had not thought of this character for years, and the name Paco was so common that he hadn't made the link.

So this was Peret's protector! No wonder the boy was afraid to come back here. Now it was all the more vital to find him and keep him away from this evil place. The child's very life might be at stake.

La Serpiente explained the situation.

'This young gentleman', she said in a voice heavy with irony, 'has taken a fancy to your Peret. He's even come all the way here to look for him. I suppose that means he's prepared to pay – but I don't really know how much. Seems a pretty shabby young gentleman to me.'

Paco stood in front of Manel, looking him up and down with contempt. Manel felt thankful that the seven years that had passed had so transformed his appearance that no-one recognized him, or they might have attacked him for having run away.

'Well,' growled Paco, 'how much? What will you give for him?'

The thought of having to pay for Peret hadn't occurred to Manel till La Serpiente broached the subject. Dare he confess that he had no money?

'I just want to speak to him.'

'That's worth money too.'

They faced each other in silence for a moment.

And then a child's voice called out from the darkness:

'Peret hasn't come back. He'll cop it when he does.'

'Shut up, you idiot,' hissed La Serpiente, while Paco made a lunge in the direction of the voice.

Manel took his chance and ran off, terrified that La Serpiente might give the word and unleash her minions from every hut. As he ran he heard the receding screams of the child, evidently being punished for telling the inconvenient truth.

It was late at night before Manel reached his part of the town. He was exhausted, discouraged, and more convinced than ever that he must somehow find Peret and keep him from ever going back to La Piedad.

Peret had spent the day dozing fitfully in his quiet corner, thinking about how he could get in touch with his friend again without going near the house where Blas was no doubt waiting to beat him to death. And, try as he might, he simply couldn't come up with a solution to the problem. The only way, as far as he could see, was to go back to the house. In the end he decided this was what he would have to do. He would wait till it was dark, till it had been dark for a long time. Then perhaps Blas would have gone to bed and he might manage to reach the room with the door and two windows without being seen. He knew it would take all the courage he could muster, to go near the place. But still, it was the only way.

He waited till nearly midnight and then ventured out into the street. He now discovered it was going to take even more courage than he had expected, for the pain from all his cuts and bruises was almost unbearable when he started walking. Besides, he felt feverish, and weak with hunger. Would he ever make it to the house? And how would his friend receive him? He must think he had disobeyed him and not waited for him to come back after work.

Stumbling and moaning quietly, Peret dragged himself on.

Wearied with his wanderings, shaken by his visit to La Piedad, and totally discouraged, Manel at last got home. On the way he had worked out a plan of campaign. He would set out early tomorrow and cover as much ground as possible in search of Peret before going to work. And he would spend every spare moment, morning and evening, just wandering about the streets, looking for his lost protégé till he found him. For surely, surely he would be bound to find him some time, somewhere?

At last he got to his room, opened the door, which he had left unlocked, and switched on the light.

A small, somewhat blood-stained figure was sitting quietly by the table.

40

Ghost Ship

'It's a ghost ship,' I said.

'Ghost? What do you mean, a ghost ship?'

'Three thousand souls – I use the expression advisedly – packed onto one ship with failing engines. Soon there'll be no food, no water . . . '

'We'll just have to put in to the nearest port.'

'The engines are failing.'

'They'll tow us in, then. We've still got radio communication, we can signal our distress.'

'They won't let us in. No port will have us.'

'Oh, come!'

'Three thousand refugees from a neighbouring state. And cholera. They simply won't let us in. What government is going to take on three thousand potential cases of cholera? I tell you, we're condemned, every one of us. Simply by being here, on this ship, we've all become untouchable.'

The very young man from the Consulate gave me a queer look and shrugged his shoulders. I could see he thought the heat had unhinged me.

Perhaps it has. The heat, and the uncertainty, and the obvious distress of all these people I'm supposed to be here to help but can do nothing for.

So perhaps this vision I so clearly see, this vision of a ghost ship, floating at random under the blazing sun, a ship covered with corpses, this vision of death and putrefaction and ominous stillness – perhaps it's nothing but a trick of my feverish brain.

That family at my feet, these people I'd have to step over if I wanted to move away, just as the young man from the Consulate stepped over them a moment ago, in a few days' time that family may have got off this floating prison, they may have moved, relieved and gladdened, down the gangway, felt the joy of the blessed earth under their feet. They may be walking the streets of a strange town, in a foreign country, whose language they cannot speak and whose culture is alien, where they have no work and no home – and yet their fate may seem blissful to them in the relief of getting off this sinister ship.

How many corpses will they have to step over, to reach that gangway?

But perhaps there will be no corpses. Perhaps the engines won't fail, food and drink will last out . . .

I try to see it happening, try to make it happen with the sheer force of my willpower. Try to see these dispossessed and frightened people disembarking quietly, hopefully, in order.

Instead I hear a shriek, see a slight commotion near the rail. Then a splash, and at the same time a chorus of cries. Someone has jumped overboard. A rope is thrown, but is pulled back after a while. There was no hand eager to cling to it.

As the dripping, useless rope is hauled back on deck, a plaintive cry is heard. Others join in, then others. Soon the whole boat is wailing, every man, woman and child, the crew, the very planks of the deck are wailing.

I wonder how the young man from the Consulate and his optimism are getting on in the midst of this lamentation. Is he wailing too?

But perhaps he doesn't hear it, perhaps he can't hear it yet.

I can hear nothing else.

Is it really happening? Already? I'm feverish, I'm imagining things. It must be the heat.

Heat can do terrible things to you. It can make you imagine the unthinkable. Like this wailing. It's inexplicable and uncanny. After all, why should they all start wailing at the same time? Only the people here, near the prow, can know about the man who went overboard. Even here, near the spot where he went over, I don't actually know what happened. Did he perhaps fall? Or did he really jump? Did he feel this sense of doom that's oppressing me, and could bear it no longer?

But why are they all lamenting, when most of them can't possibly know what happened? Have they some sort of collective means of knowing, some faculty we are too sophisticated and too civilized to have retained?

Or are they simply giving vent to their sense of the unbearableness of their situation? Parched, hungry, disease ridden, scorched by the pitiless sun, with no water, no shelter, no room to move, and the growing conviction that the ship will never reach port, that they will float aimlessly about this blazing ocean for ever and ever with nothing, absolutely nothing to hope for.

I step across the family in front of me, struggle to the nearest rail and grasp it. The metal is so hot it nearly burns my hands but I refuse to let go – I must have something to hold on to. And so I cling on, fiercely, furiously, using every atom of strength in the effort.

And the wailing stops.

Did it ever begin?

The water is very quiet, very smooth, almost oily. We slide through so slowly that we seem to raise hardly a ripple. But even the water seems hostile, for the rays of light it sends back are as dazzling as the sun itself. Long, bright daggers, piercing straight through your eyes to your very brain.

I close my eyes, but the daggers are still there, thrusting deeper and deeper into my tormented brain.

So I struggle back to where I was before, carefully stepping over the family I had beside me. The mother is in the same position as before, sitting on the deck, holding a small child in her arms. The child has stopped crying and whimpering now, and lies very still. Sleep at last, I think, and feel some relief. The mother sits absolutely still, as if afraid to move and disturb the infant.

After a while I begin to worry about the child's immobility. And the mother's stillness is equally marked.

Half an hour later neither of them has moved. The child, I am now convinced, is dead. Does the mother know? I wait there, dreading the moment of realization, bracing myself against the cry of anguish that must follow.

But there is to be no cry. Instead, I see the mother's black, shiny cheeks are streaked by a flow of silent tears. She knows. She is cradling her child for the last time.

Another cry is heard, coming from amidships, then a splash. Then more cries and more splashes. It's as if a suicidal fever had suddenly possessed the passengers, who fling themselves overboard, one after another. No one even bothers to throw a line. A fatalistic apathy has taken over.

And one after another, as if at a signal, more and more people jump into the water, seeking salvation from the intolerable conditions on board. At least the water's cool, at least it's wet.

I abandon the afflicted family and make for the rail again. No need to struggle to get there this time. There are as many people in the water as on deck by now.

And the daggers from the sea are not striking any more, for the sea is no longer a dazzling mirror. The sea has turned black, black with the countless bodies floating in it, beautiful black bodies, with strong, shining limbs, rising, falling, before they finally sink and their place is taken by yet more.

I close my eyes and see what the deck will soon look like – empty, bare, except for the few possessions the people have left behind as they get up and take their place by the rail, waiting for their turn to jump over. And the pathos of these few, poor belongings, which only a few days ago had seemed precious enough to be dragged into exile, is greater than the huddled presence of their owners was only a few minutes ago.

At last I open my eyes. The deck is crowded as before. In front of me I see the woman cradling her dead child, still motionless, impassive. Even the tears have stopped flowing. She is a stone, a statue. And her companions have also been turned to stone, silent, motionless.

The whole deck is covered by these impressive sculptures in jet. I look around in all directions and see nothing but corpses. I wonder about the very young man from the Consulate. Is he dead too? And the captain? I walk up and down the deck, carefully avoiding the outstretched limbs – black, shining, beautiful – and I can find no sign of life.

And the silence is complete, immeasurable. The engines have given their last, faint, inadequate *put-put* and fallen silent. The ship, with its load of dead flesh, looks vast, immovable. For ever and for ever and for ever it will stay here, just here, where nothing can move it, where no-one will find it, with its black, perishable cargo.

There are no bodies floating in the sea. They are all here, on deck. I acknowledge my hallucination. All those suicides, they happened in my head, only there. Except, perhaps, for that first victim who surrendered to his fear and despair. The others sat it out – and fared no better. The ship is black and heavy with their dead.

Once again the illusion fades. I see the corpses are alive – alive, and still enduring the unendurable – the heat, the thirst, the hunger, the fear, the homelessness. The waiting.

The captain stands beside me.

'You'll be all right now,' he says.

'Yes, yes, I'm quite all right. It's these people, these poor people . . . Can nothing be done for them?'

'They'll be all right, you'll see. They have a great capacity for endurance, greater than ours. The cholera will claim a few, the rest will cope.'

'One of them didn't,' I say. 'One of them jumped overboard, didn't he?'

'Oh, that?' A shadow passes over the captain's face. 'That wasn't one of them. That was one of us, who just couldn't take it. A young man from the Consulate.'

41

On Home Ground

I'm here, standing in my kitchen, gazing out of the window. Inside, the room is warm and glowing with the blaze of the fire. Outside, I see nothing but grey. Mist and cloud, the grey of the farm buildings, the grey outline of a tree just beyond the yard. Not a leaf, not a blade of grass to cast a green blessing over the place. It's winter.

But that's all right. I don't mind winter, I don't mind grey. It's a soft colour, a kind colour, that steps back to let the summer greens and reds and yellows take pride of place. And when winter has washed away all the bright warm shades, and there's nothing but grey left, grey on grey, that's when you truly see the world about you, its shape, its outline. That's when you really know where you are.

So, I have this kitchen. A little ship of warmth and colour floating in this soft grey sea. The pale pine table, scrubbed clean and spotless. The two armchairs – a little shabby, but the colours still fairly strong. The stone floor with the old hearth rug, also past its best, but still good for another year or two. The dresser, solid, dependable, not to be moved, housing my porcelain treasures. And the fire in the hearth.

Permanence, that's what this room speaks of. Little has changed since I first walked in, as a young bride twenty years ago. Even then, that very first day, I knew my roots were here. A sense of homecoming. The world was cold and bleak outside, for it was November, with all of winter waiting at the door. But inside! Oh, inside was this island of warmth and light. Home, my home, to share with John.

Tinkers, that's what they used to call my family. Father preferred to describe himself as an itinerant farm worker. He'd had a good education, even gone to university. Wanted to be a lawyer, like his own father. It was the drink that finished him. By the time I was born – I was the fifth – he'd gone tumbling down the social ladder to reach rock bottom. Itinerant farm worker, or, if you prefer it, tinker.

It took me a long time to work out why they called me Last Straw. My mother had managed to cope – just – with a drunken husband, no regular income, and four brats. They were short of money, they were short of everything. The one thing they never seemed to run out of was drink. And one day, when my mother was too tired and too harried and too depressed to cope with us all – me, months old, screaming my head off most of the time – she raided my father's pockets while he lay happily snoring on the floor, found a half-bottle of whisky, and decided this was to be her comfort in future. Oh, she knew what she was doing, she had my father's example. Many years later, in one of her sober moments, she told me she had been faced with the choice of death or degradation. For she knew that, unless she found some comfort, some relief, she would have thrown herself over the nearest cliff. And then who would have taken care of us children?

After that, whenever I reproached her for her drinking, she would say:

'Just you remember this, I took to the bottle for your sake.'

By the time I was born they'd given up even trying to run a permanent home.

At eighteen I had never lived more than a few months in the same place. I thought of myself as a feather, blown hither and thither by the wind. A feather or a straw – for wasn't that what they called me? The Last Straw.

And then I met John at a fair and he fell in love with me right away. No, I didn't love him, not in the falling-in-love sort of way. But I liked him and admired him, and felt ready to give him all my devotion in return for the kind of stability he was offering.

And that's why this farm cottage, looking out to the farmyard on one side, and the moors on the other, has always seemed like heaven to me, and I've felt at home here from the very first day. Rooted.

But there's more to it than that. Yes, much more.

There's this feeling of belonging. Not just at the present moment. Oh no, it goes a long way further back. I felt as if I'd always lived here. Long, long before I was born, I mean. When I walked into this cottage, even though I'd never seen it before, I knew I'd come home. Not just from my endless wanderings, though that, of course, meant a lot to me. But it wasn't just this home that would now be mine.

Recognition, that's the only word to describe what I

felt. That first day I stood in the doorway and looked out at what was to be my landscape from then on. And I knew I had come home. I knew these moors, I knew this skyline. They had been mine from time immemorial.

I tried to tell John what I felt.

'Come home?' he said. 'Of course you have. I've been getting this house ready for you for the last three months, praying you would like it when you came.'

'I do, I do, I love everything about it.'

He has never understood me – not about my sense of coming home. Twenty years later, I can still say that. For years I was too busy to think about it. Running my little house, doing domestic work in the farmhouse, looking after John and the children . . . I had no time to think of anything. But it was there, the feeling deep down, this conviction that this was where I belonged, where I had always belonged. That I was on home ground.

I don't know why, but now this has become the most important thing in my life. Perhaps because the children have grown up and left home, and I don't work at the farmhouse any more. A ploughman's pay is all we need for the two of us.

So I have this wonderful thing called leisure. And all the thoughts that were lying sleepily at the back of my mind have roused themselves and come creeping to the front, waiting for me to acknowledge them.

It has been a deep pleasure, a great indulgence, to get to know these long-dormant thoughts, to listen to the voices. And so I have become acquainted with my former companions.

There's Kate. She was the first I heard.

Kate. 'Time to get up. It's always time to get up. And my bones are so weary, the voice mumbled. But I hear my mother in the kitchen, lighting the fire, and that means I should be up too. And if I'm not in the kitchen by the time my father comes through, there'll be trouble. I know all about that – trouble. Bruises and a black eye. And I don't want another of those, not with the new shepherd likely to pass this way with his flock.

He's called Campbell and he's very nice. Quite old, really – must be forty at least. But still . . . Always very solemn, though. I'd like to see him smile, to see him smile at me.

The first time I saw him I thought he looked a bit stern. And I didn't really like that. I like people to laugh and smile and make me feel happy. I get enough stern looks at home.

Well, I still haven't seen him smiling, and yet it doesn't really matter, somehow. I could listen to him all day. It's his voice, and the things he says, too. For he speaks to me now; in a quiet, earnest way, as if I counted.

The first time we spoke I felt really awkward. He'd come to see my father about one of the dykes which was in a bad way, letting the sheep through, and Father wasn't back from market yet. And Mother was busy in the kitchen, so I had him to myself for a few minutes. I didn't know what to say, and the silence made me nervous. He just sat quietly, looking out of the window, and I could see he wasn't nervous in the least. I spoke at last, for I couldn't bear the silence any longer, and I said the first thing that came into my head, which was what I'd been wondering about him ever since he came:

'Don't you get lonely on the hill all day, by yourself?'

He turned his head and looked at me steadily; and he took so long to reply I thought he wasn't going to.

'No, I don't get lonely. Why should I?'

'Because you've no-one to talk to.'

'No-one else to talk to, you mean.'

I stared at him – gaped at him, more likely, with my mouth hanging open in surprise.

'No-one else? But there's no-one there!'

'Oh yes, there's me. I'm there all the time.'

Seeing I was completely perplexed, he went on:

'I talk to myself. Don't you? Talk to yourself, I mean.'

'Of course not! I'm not daft. Only mad people talk to themselves.' Then, realizing I seemed to be calling him mad, I turned scarlet and didn't know where to look.

But he didn't seem to mind. In the same quiet, untroubled tone, he continued:

'You're wrong, you know. Most people talk to themselves most of the time, though not aloud. You probably do it too.'

The door opened and my father walked into the room.

'What's this about a dyke falling to bits?' He sounded, as usual, cross.

I escaped . . . .

For days I wondered and worried about this business of talking to myself. Did I really do it? I longed to meet the shepherd again and ask him about it, and yet I knew in my heart I simply wouldn't dare.

And then one day, just as I was crossing the farmyard, there he was. I know I blushed and looked away, chiding myself for my lack of courage.

But I needn't have worried, for it was he who spoke.

'Well, Kate, are you still talking to yourself?'

'I . . . I haven't started. I don't know what you mean.'

'Talking to yourself inside, I mean. That's what your thoughts are, a conversation with yourself. For you do have thoughts, don't you?'

I nodded, and blushed again.

'Don't worry, I'm not going to ask you what those thoughts are. I just want to ask you to listen to them, those voices inside you. They're the most important thing you'll ever hear.'

Well, I started listening to the voices then, and what they said was that Campbell was the most amazing and wonderful man I'd ever met in the whole sixteen years of my life.

He told me so many things – about the past and about this place and how the people lived, working in the lead mines.

'What lead mines? There's no lead mines here!'

'Not now. But there were, long ago. Instead of running a farm, your father probably would have been down the mine.'

'When was this?'

'Oh, centuries ago. And this whole area, instead of moorland, was under forest.'

'But how do you know?'

'I've read about it, and you can see it in the landscape. It's not been like this for ever. The land makes us what we are, but we in turn change it – cutting down trees, altering the course of a stream or even a river. It's a two-way business, like what goes on inside your head, with all those voices.'

I pondered for a little. Then:

'Is everything a two-way business?' I asked.

And he smiled. For the first time I saw him smiling.

'Good girl, Kate. You've got the message. Now I can let you go. You'll be all right now.' And he looked solemn again.

What did he mean, about letting me go? I wondered.

The following week I heard he was leaving, and the whole world turned black for me. That was when I knew I was in love with him. He was three times my age, and yet I was in love with him. And he was going away!

He came to see me just before leaving.

I wanted to plead with him, to beg him to stay. Instead all I could say was:

'You're lucky, going away to see new places. I'm stuck here. There's no way I can get away. You're lucky.'

'You still have a lot to discover here, Kate.'

'Without you?' And I can still feel the cry of reproach deep inside me as the words were torn from me.

'Certainly, without me. You've got the key, and I must move on. It's the best thing I can do for you, Kate.'

He looked at me steadily, serenely, as he spoke. Suddenly it struck me that he had guessed my feelings for him, and this was why he was leaving. It wasn't till years later that it occurred to me that perhaps his feelings too were involved, and he knew, as even I knew at the time, that this could lead to nothing but disaster.

I never saw him again. And yet no-one has ever remained so close to me. For he gave me this landscape and its history, and the love of place, which I now see has been the most abiding thing in my life.

Yes, I got quite fond of Kate. I felt, in a way, that I had

grown up with her, as I learned more and more about these hills and moors, and felt their power inside me.

Then there was Martin.

I first heard his voice as a series of curses echoing through the lead mine. He was cursing the rock that had just fallen on his foot, and cursing his mate for his carelessness in letting the rock fall. He was cursing the long walk back to the surface – long and difficult and painful, dragging his broken foot along. And he was cursing the prospect of several weeks off work while he recovered – and who was going to bring in the money to buy food for the family?

Gradually Martin's curses subsided. From his monologue I learned that in time he came to accept the loss of his foot, the knowledge that he'd never again be fit to do a day's work – not what he and his people considered proper work, down the mines.

And so he took to reading. He read, again and again, the few books he could find – the Bible, *Pilgrim's Progress*, Culpeper's *Complete Herbal*, till reading became a pleasure instead of a torment. He worked hard at the even more arduous mysteries of handwriting. And, because he felt he himself had nothing worth saying, he copied out page after page of his books. I would hear his voice laboriously reading out each syllable he wrote:

Arch-an-gel. To put a gloss up-on their prac-tice, the phy-sy-cians call an herb (which coun-try peo-ple vul-gar-ly know by the name of the dead nett-le) arch-an-gel . . .

Yes, the cursing had stopped. And he was never bored, for people came to consult him about all their ailments.

'Yes, I see. Now, let's see what Culpeper says . . . '

Martin too had found his roots in the place. He could no longer wander about the hills, but he knew every plant that grows there, he knew its properties and its virtues. He knew that he and they were all part of the same thing, this bleak little corner of the earth where they all belonged.

And then there were the voices of the foresters, whispering, rustling voices, mingled with the murmur of the leaves and the sough of the branches . . .

Under the beech tree, where the branches dip down to make a bower . . . Yes, he led me there and we sat down . . . well, yes, we lay down . . . his hands . . .

And all day we worked together in the forest, with the others, me and Tommy, as if he was nothing to me and I nothing to him, waiting for the night.

The storm that day . . . it came so sudden, we all had to stop work and take shelter in the hut at the far end of Leaning Wood.

Too near the oak, the Centuries Oak. It can't stand for ever, and in a gale like this . . . and the lightning too, we should be out in the open.

Right then, you men, you can go out into the open, and catch your death in this downpour. I'm staying here, in the hut, with the children and the rest of the women-folk.

But the oak . . . Can't you see, the way the wind's blowing, we're right in its path!

I'll say a prayer to the oak, it'll protect us . . .

Heathen! You'd be better praying to the Lord Jesus Christ!

And then a few screams and a great crash, and the voices were silent.

Later, much later, the girl's voice again . . .

Yes, the beech tree, the beech tree . . . That's where my happiness started. So few nights, lying in the shelter of the beech tree. And then the oak, the Centuries Oak, came along – for that's what it did, it rushed across and crashed down and killed him. My Tommy, my hope and my happiness . . .

Trees, trees, our whole life is bound up with them, they rule our world. They make you toil day after day for your living, they shade you and shelter you, and then they crush your dreams, and leave nothing but a mangled, lifeless body, in a tangle of broken branches and dead leaves . . .

Dead leaves, and broken branches . . .

And here, standing in my warm, welcoming kitchen, looking out over the desolate hills, I hear voices that go even further back, voices that say few words, coming from an echoing world of stone . . .

And I wonder if some lone man or woman in these bleak uplands will some day hear my voice, mingled with these others that have come to me, and feel this same sense of belonging, this same sense of continuing, of being part of an enduring whole. And feel rooted in the soil and in the centuries.

42

No time for donkeys

As he passed the little boy leading his donkey, the man smiled at him. And the boy, who was looking up, waiting for the smile, bowed gravely to the tall figure.

This was their normal communication. They had never exchanged a word. And yet, neither would have hesitated in describing the other as his friend.

Yes, he is my friend, this boy, one of the benign influences in my life. The donkey too – another friend.

After a few yards the priest stopped and turned to look at the boy as he retreated along the track with his donkey. The cloud of dust in which they moved was lit up by the slanting rays of the early morning sun.

Like a halo. The dust, the humble dust, blessing the simple boy and his beast as they pass, enriching my life.

He smiled again as he thought of how different his life had been. So much noise inside, so much noise outside. And now the sight of this boy with his donkey could fill him with such calm, such content.

Years ago I simply wouldn't have seen the pair; or else, if I had actually become aware of their presence, it would only have been as a possible obstacle, something that might at some time get in my way. I had so much to do, so little time to do it in. There was no room for obstacles in my life, no time for donkeys.

He had been one of the outstanding young men of his generation. His parents had been poor, and their son had done what most gifted and ambitious boys of humble origin had to do last century in Spain – discover a vocation that gave them entry to a seminary, thus opening the only possible door that would lead to a decent education.

For this young man there were no real problems in accepting the life of a priest. He was of a serious and scholarly nature, and felt that embracing a life of poverty and chastity would be a small price to pay for the inestimable advantages of access to a good education, books, serious discussion. As a member of the Jesuit Order he looked forward to a quiet life of teaching, with plenty of time left for private study.

But his Order soon discovered his gift for argument, his ability to convince, to raise enthusiasm with his mastery of impressive words and well placed rhetorical devices. Before long he was being sent on one mission after another, travelling the length and breadth of the country, arguing, convincing, persuading the rich and powerful to save their souls and, at the same time, society in general, by means of generous donations.

'My friends, I have some serious and solemn words to say to you. Words of encouragement, but also of reproach. And the words you are about to hear do not come from myself, not from my own humble, limited knowledge, but rather from an infinitely higher source. And what I have to say to you is this—' Father Eusebi paused for dramatic effect; and as he drew in a breath for his next sentence, a donkey just outside the window near where the orator was standing began to bray. It was a powerful bray, full of the infinite sadness and despair that a donkey's voice can convey, and it went on and on, each note linked to the other with no pause in between.

Father Eusebi had met many a doughty adversary in the oratorical lists, and had seldom been vanquished, and never routed. But this deafening, desolated braying was more than he could cope with. His audience sat still, in respectful silence, waiting for the nuisance to abate; but the priest felt certain he sensed a wave of suppressed merriment ripple through the assembled hearers. The donkey's timing had been impeccable, replacing the words of loving reproach that the holy father had just promised.

Confused and shaken, he waited in silence for the noise to subside. But the donkey seemed to be speaking for all of its kind, through all the generations of their captivity, and its anguish did not abate. Eventually someone was sent off to lead the animal away, still pouring forth its grief.

Father Eusebi resumed his speech. But he could remember none of the fine phrases he had prepared; and his usual gift for improvisation deserted him. He struggled through to the end, aware that his audience were counting the minutes till they could be free of him and burst out laughing.

And as he struggled for words (the very first time in his twenty years of preaching that the right words had not come winging to him from the heavens), he was telling himself that he had bungled it, that what he should have done was laugh, and allow his hearers to laugh too. Then he could have started again – perhaps less grandiloquently than originally intended, but at least in a less inhibited manner, and with a more willing audience.

After he had stumbled to the end of his ordeal he left the room and made his way to the stables, where he felt sure the donkey had been led. And there he found it, standing stolidly, immobile, with its head drooping, silent at last.

As the priest came up to it the donkey looked up, and man and beast stared at each other for a while.

'Do you realize what you've done, you witless animal? A lot depended on today's address, and you've ruined it all. We won't get any of the splendid results we were expecting, and it's all your fault.'

The donkey drew its ears back, as if rejecting the accusation.

'So, what have you to say for yourself?'

The animal raised its head, with its upper lip lifted, revealing a row of long, yellow teeth. It seemed to be expressing scorn.

Father Eusebi was beginning to resent his opponent's silence. All right, it was only an animal, but still, the priest was not used to having his arguments greeted with total silence. It seemed to put his adversary in a position of superiority. And when the adversary in question was only a donkey, and one that had shown itself capable of sustained discourse . . .

On his way back to his own seminary he found it impossible to forget the incident. He would have to report back to his superior and confess the failure of this particular mission. And there would be no point in laying too much stress on the animal's participation in the event. He knew what he would be told, what he had been telling himself ever since the incident occurred – that he should not have allowed a stupid little thing like that to prevent him from preaching the Word of God and pointing out the exact manner in which God's will could best be served in this particular instance.

He found himself going over the expected conversation, finding plenty of telling words to put in his superior's mouth, and very few effective ones with which to counter the other man's reproaches.

As he sat in the train, gazing out at the flat, arid landscape around him, he became aware for the first time of how many donkeys were to be seen taking their share in the humble tasks of the peasants. It occurred to him that he had never seriously looked at a donkey before in his life. Awkward animals, lacking the elegance of the horse and the strength of the ox. Yet the good Lord had seen fit to create them.

He turned away from the sight of them in some distaste, and gradually sank into a lethargy that was neither sleep nor waking. And in this half-waking state he began a conversation with that morning's donkey.

I told you, and I meant it, that you had ruined my whole expedition. What have you to say for yourself?

Nothing much. Certainly a lot less than you've always got to say for yourself.

You needn't be so disrespectful. And it's not true, anyway. I have very little to say for myself.

Nonsense! You never stop talking.

That's different. What I say is not for myself; I am spreading the Word of God.

Trying to get more money for your seminary, you mean?

That is only incidental. Most of my time is spent defending the sacred dogmas of the Church. What higher calling could there be? I am the humble mouthpiece of the Lord.

Well, I must say, he's rather verbose, your Lord is. Why does he need to use so many words?

You're just jealous, because you can't use words at all.

You'll not deny I was eloquent, all the same, was I not?

At this point Father Eusebi interrupted his imaginary conversation. He remembered the sorrow, the anguish that had seemed to vibrate in the animal's voice, and felt it like a wound in his own flesh. Yes, the donkey had been eloquent. Its endless, harsh and sobbing bray had dragged the lofty preacher down to earth. The donkey, in its prolonged, anguished outpouring, he now realized, seemed to be speaking for the whole of its kind, and for lost, sorrowing humankind as well. The priest now saw that his own discomfiture had been caused not just by the absurdity of the interruption, but by the earthiness of the emotion in the animal's lament.

It was a question of values, he now saw. So far he had prized only the things of the spirit and, perhaps more so, the things of the intellect. The donkey's mournful cry had brought him face to face at last with the anguished protest of suffering flesh. The sound had no intellectual content, so there was no arguing against it; its spiritual value would have been hard to define; aesthetically it was a disaster. And yet it had stirred him more deeply than he could have believed possible.

Where does that leave me? he wondered. Here is a completely new level I shall have to take into account from now on. Where do all my fine words belong in this new scheme of things?

From that day on he was torn between his desire to continue with his usual work, making his deadly attacks on evil, indifference and unsound dogma, and the knowledge that he could no longer go on ignoring this new aspect of life that had been revealed to him.

So far he had drawn a straight and clear-cut line between humanity and the animal kingdom. And now this donkey had spoken for them all, of that he was convinced, uniting all living creatures in one bond of servitude and suffering.

He continued with his preaching, with his endless, learned discussions. But he seemed to have lost his flair. Gradually he was replaced by other, younger, more dynamic men on the important missions. In a way this was a relief, for his heart was no longer in his work. The new dimension that had come into his life was engaging too much of his thought for him to desire the constant coming and going, the endless social gatherings that had taken up his time before.

The one thing he missed was making up his speeches. He had always loved playing with words, choosing them carefully for effect, highlighting the most special ones, putting them together in wonderful, dazzling figures of speech. This he missed enormously at first, as his need of words diminished with his reduced workload.

And then, one day, as he meditated on the imaginary conversation he had had with the donkey that day in the train, he remembered how he had made the donkey accuse the Almighty of being verbose, of using too many words.

I didn't really mean it at the time, I was just playing devil's advocate. But still . . . Perhaps the morning's
incident had shocked me into a state of unusual men-
tal clarity. And, of course, the Almighty himself uses no
words; but, as his humble interpreter, perhaps *I* was using
too many.

Gradually he came to the conclusion that words were
too precious to be used in such profusion. Words were
jewels, he now saw, to be used sparingly, lovingly; with
reverence.

In his later years, as he withdrew more and more from
the life of the seminary, he adopted the habit of allow-
ing himself a special word every day. One word, one
word only, to repeat, to savour, examining its etymology,
remembering passages in scripture, in theological works,
in the classics, where this word had been used. This was
his one indulgence. For the rest, he gave himself to the
cultivation of silence.

As the boy's figure disappeared in the distance Father
Eusebi turned and resumed his walk and his meditation
on that day's word.

Caryatid.

Yes, a good word, caryatid. From the Greek, of course.
Karuatides, priestesses of Artemis at Karuai. For a moment he let his imagination people the austere, dusty and
familiar landscape with a long row of draped female
figures, crowned with highly ornate Corinthian capitals,
supporting the roof of an endless colonnade which disappeared into the distance. And he thought with immense
satisfaction of the fantastic difference that one word had
made to his view of the landscape – and to his own

inner landscape as well. Long ago that one magical word would have passed unperceived in the welter of other equally fine words that were continually swimming in his mind. The landscape would have remained bare, austere, totally everyday. Now, isolated, the word had produced this vision of an impossible but fascinating addition to the familiar scene. He stood still, with his eyes closed, taking in the landscape with its fanciful addition. Would it, could it ever be like this, peopled by caryatids? Or had this vision come to him from some remote past? When the Romans were here, perhaps?

Priestesses, that's what they were supposed to represent, the caryatids. Just imagine this place overrun by priestesses. Perish the thought!

Smiling indulgently at the pagan notion, he opened his eyes, determined to see things as they were. He looked behind him, to see whether the boy and the donkey were still in sight, but they had disappeared. Looking ahead he saw nothing but the dusty road advancing over the bare plain.

Caryatid.

The word came into his mind yet again, like a silver ball dropping into a limpid pool, sending shimmering ripples right across the surface.

That road, now. Something odd about it.

It's only the light, he told himself, just a ray of light dancing along by the side of the road. But he could have sworn he saw ahead of him, faint and shimmering, a glorious colonnade of caryatids.

And he smiled again, as he thought of the boy leading his humble donkey past these imposing classical figures.

43

Gentle Hills

Every time she walked along the low road she could feel the hills on either side moving along peacefully beside her. An illusion, she knew. The two rows of hills were so evenly balanced – the ones to the east a little higher and further off; the ones to the west nearer and lower. And the outlines of the two ridges were almost identical.

Gentle hills, she always felt, peaceful and gentle. Nowhere else did she feel so at one with her surroundings, so secure.

Green velvet, soft and smooth.

Moira Maxwell had spent most of her life in Edinburgh. And then one day, to everyone's surprise, she sold her flat and set off for the Southern Uplands, leaving the comfort and apparent security of Newington behind.

She wanted peace and silence, and felt she had got it right, having chosen her hills carefully. The house itself was of little concern to her. So long as the hills, her neighbours, were right, that was all that mattered. And these hills, broad-based, solid, not too high, polished smooth by glaciation, were just what she wanted. No wild Romantic landscape; but a friendly gathering of quiet, companionable hills. Yes, quiet upland hills these, sweetly merging into one another to form a long, gentle outline. And this favourite walk, with the two rows of hills, each a mirror image of the other . . . Oh, it was lovely, enchanting, almost hypnotic! Walking along with the hills moving along beside you . . . You just went on and on, and there they were, beside you all the way, your companions.

The hills, she felt sure, helped her with her problem. They were the antidote to the constant sense of oppression that had driven her from the city. For in Edinburgh she felt the weight of every stone, every brick, in all those buildings. Oppressed and tangled, that's how she felt. Oppressed by the weight of all that displaced matter that formed the buildings, confused by the random, ceaseless activity all about her. Looking out of her third-floor window, watching the traffic, she was always aware of the tangle of the innumerable paths traced by the passing vehicles. She imagined that each car was trailing a long ribbon after it, and these ribbons became inextricably knotted and twisted as the cars turned to left or right, as they overtook each other or drew in to park. She longed for something smooth and simple and continuous.

And the weight of all those buildings! Even in her own flat she constantly felt this. Above her, the fourth floor weighed her down, and she could never forget her own weight added to that of her flat, on the two floors below. And all this rested on a honeycomb of tunnels, channels, subterranean chambers to supply the needs of the whole community! When she heard of the underground streets in the Old Town her fear grew even more urgent. What if the crumbling remains of a yet undiscovered street lay right beneath her very building?

This phobia was beginning to interfere with her friendships. She began to avoid the town centre, and had to make up excuses for not meeting her friends there.

Since leaving school Moira had spent one evening a week with her friend Julia. A rigid rota had been established, with each visiting the other's house weekabout. This had worked very well till Julia moved out of Newington and bought a house in Gilmerton, in a nice little modern estate, with a small garden in need of attention.

Moira was delighted, and even helped out with the digging.

And then one day, as they sat at their meal looking out over the results of their labours, Julia said:

'Did you know that this used to be a mining area? This very house, I've only just discovered, is built right on top of a disused mine. I find it rather romantic – don't you?'

Moira found it profoundly disturbing.

'I mean,' went on Julia, 'I imagine the ghosts of all those miners chipping away at the coalface. And I see the coal being carried up to the surface by those poor girls with creels on their backs. And I think, thank goodness all that's over, and the poor things are now resting in peace.'

After that, resting in peace was the last thing Moira was able to do in Julia's house.

She simply couldn't face another evening in that precarious dwelling, and knew she would have to find some excuse for not going back, while hoping Julia would never be plunged, along with her desirable residence, into the bowels of the earth.

For some time she solved the problem with a twisted ankle. It wasn't badly twisted, but she was able to get a lot of mileage out of it.

'Simply can't drive, dear,' she explained. 'You had better come to me, if you don't mind.'

Julia didn't mind – not for quite a few weeks. Then she noticed that Moira was at times forgetting to limp.

'Don't you think it's about time you started coming back to my place? What's keeping you?'

'It's this ankle. It's still bothering me. I haven't driven for weeks.'

Julia looked sceptical, then said:

'All right, then. I'll come for you.'

Moira turned pale and could find nothing to say.

'You just don't want to come, do you?'

'Yes, yes, of course. It's just . . . '

'Just what?'

'Just that . . . Oh, I can't explain.'

And she couldn't.

In the end the weekly meeting was abandoned.

Moira was upset at the loss of her oldest friend, in spite of her relief at not having to go back to that dangerous house.

But she still had the problem of the network of underground passages honeycombing the whole city. And the weight, the weight of it all!

It was too much; and, having lost touch with her oldest friend, she decided to move away from this mass of fears and irritations.

* * *

Living in the country was balm to her spirit. The ground beneath her, she knew, was rock-solid. There was virtually no traffic – just the odd tractor rattling along, a few cars driven by the local farmers, an occasional pick-up with a bleating sheep in the back. All very soothing, like a cool, gentle wave flowing over you on a hot, sticky day.

She soon became friendly with her next-door neighbour, Nell. One day, as they chatted over the garden fence, Nell confessed that she was finding it difficult to keep the garden in order.

'It's the digging,' she said. 'I've got a bad back, and I can't cope with the digging.'

'I enjoy it,' announced Moira. 'I used to help a friend in Edinburgh with her garden, and I loved the digging. Gives you such a sense of achievement.'

'What it gives me is a pain in the . . . back.'

Moira laughed, and offered to do the heavy work in Nell's garden.

The friendship flourished, and so did both gardens.

'Do you talk to your plants?' Moira asked one day.

'Oh yes, of course. All good gardeners do.'

Moira smiled, contented. Some day, perhaps, she would tell her friend that she talked to her hills, that they accompanied her as she walked along. This was such a precious conviction (or rather, illusion, she reminded herself) that she would have liked to share it with somebody.

Through Nell she met her cousin, Alice, who had a more vigorous and sceptical turn of mind. At first Moira found her rather intimidating.

'Can't imagine why anyone would leave the city to

come and live in a barren wilderness like this!' Alice exclaimed.

'Well then, why do you stay here?' Moira inquired.

'It's my husband's job. Not many shepherds required in the city, you know.'

Moira had to agree. Nell explained later that Alice had made a mistake in marrying a shepherd, as she was very intelligent and had had a good education. 'Like the rest of us,' she added.

As time went on Moira came to enjoy her conversations with the redoubtable Alice, and told her of her real reasons for leaving Edinburgh.

'It wasn't just that I wanted peace and quiet. Well, yes, I did, but that wasn't all. It was the weight, the sheer weight of it all.'

'I know exactly what you mean,' stated Alice in her emphatic way. 'Personally, of course, I love the hurry and bustle of city life. But for anyone who doesn't, I see it could take the form of an actual physical burden, weighing you down.'

'That's not really what I mean. It's not that I feel the dislike as a weight. It's the actual material weight of all those buildings. I feel crushed by them all.'

Alice looked at her attentively, then said:

'I'm sure there's a name for it.'

'For what?'

'For this type of phobia.'

'Oh!'

Moira decided against mentioning her conviction that the whole city was in danger of collapsing. Perhaps Alice thought there was a name for that too!

Alice was still intent on finding the right label for her

friend's phobia.

'How about "ponderophobia"?' she suggested. Seeing a blank look on Moira's face, she explained, 'From the Latin *pondus, ponderis*, meaning weight. Or perhaps something from *onus, oneris*, a burden. For you did feel the weight as a burden, didn't you?'

'Ye-es, I suppose so. Most people feel weight as a burden, don't you think?'

'No doubt I feel my extra stone and a half very much as a burden. But that's not a phobia, you understand.'

'I understand. I'm the one with the phobia.'

'And I'm the one with the burden of extra weight.'

'Well, at least you can easily do something about your problem.'

'Eat less, you mean? Not as easy as you might think.' Then, after moment's pause, Alice added, 'Still, easier to cope with than a phobia, I suppose. There's not much you can do about that.'

'I have.'

'You have what?'

'Done something about it. I've come here.'

'And the problem has disappeared?'

'Completely.'

'But what about all these hills? Surely they must weigh a lot more than all the buildings of Edinburgh piled one on top of another?'

Moira shuddered at the image. 'No, the hills are all right. They're in their own proper place. We haven't shifted them.' They shift themselves, though, she thought, when we're out walking together. I wonder what she'd say if I told her that? But no, Alice was not the right listener for this sort of revelation.

A few days later she tackled Nell instead, approaching the subject in a roundabout way:

'Nell, when you talk to your flowers, what is it you say to them?'

'I tell them how lovely they are.'

'Does Alice know you talk to your flowers?'

'Alice? I suppose so. Everyone knows that gardeners talk to their flowers. Don't you talk to yours?'

This was the opening Moira had been hoping for:

'Yes. But then, I talk to other things too.'

'Some people do. I know a lady who talks to her favourite kitchen knife. She says it keeps it sharp. Absurd, isn't it?'

'Is it any more absurd than what we do? Talking to our plants?'

'Not the same thing at all. The plants are alive. They respond by blooming and blossoming and looking gorgeous.'

'So it's all right if you talk to a living thing, you mean?'

'Absolutely.'

Moira wondered whether the hills could qualify as living things.

'I sometimes talk to my . . . to the hills,' she ventured.

Nell was obviously giving the matter some consideration.

'Well, yes. They too are living things, in a manner of speaking. Geologically speaking, I mean. After all, they evolve in time. If you give them long enough, that is. Tectonic forces, they call it. You know, volcanos and earthquakes and glaciation. All that.'

'Yes,' agreed Moira, not sure this technical approach

192

was necessary. Still, it did mean that Nell was sympathetic to the way she felt about her beloved hills, since she conceded they were alive.

'Sometimes,' she went on, 'when I'm walking along the valley road, I feel the hills on both sides are walking along beside me, keeping me company.'

A startled look from Nell made her add hastily:

'It's only a sensation, you know. A sort of optical illusion, if you like. I know the hills can't get up and walk.'

'No, they can't.' Nell sounded quite sharp. 'Not even to accompany a devotee like you. But there's no harm in imagining it, is there?' she added placatingly.

No more was said on the subject, but Moira was left feeling uneasy. Would Nell tell her cousin? She wished she hadn't spoken.

That evening Nell went round to Alice's house.

'Well, Nell, what brings you out at this ungodly hour? Central heating broken down?'

'I shall disregard your offensive innuendo. I've come to see you about Moira.'

'And what has Moira *done* to you? For you don't go and see someone about someone else unless there's something *wrong*. So what *is* it?'

'It's just something she said– about the hills. *Her* hills, she called them, then changed it to *the* hills.'

'So what? She just feels a little possessive about them. Newcomers do. Especially those whose husbands don't have to go tramping all over said hills looking for lost sheep.'

'It's more than that. It's what she said about them.' Nell paused.

'Well?'

'She said that when she goes for a walk along the valley road, the hills walk with her. Keeping her company, she said.'

'She said the hills *actually* walk with her?'

'That's the impression she gave me. But when she saw the look on my face she back-pedalled, saying something about its being only an illusion. But the problem is, I'm sure that wasn't what she really meant. I got the impression she really thought that was what was happening. Or at least, that's what she wanted it to be like.'

Alice was looking thoughtful. Then she asked:

'Did she say anything about being bothered by weight?'

'Weight? Her? She's as thin as a rake!'

'No, not that sort of weight. The weight of buildings.'

'What buildings?'

'All the buildings in Edinburgh.'

'The . . . ! Alice, what on earth are you talking about?'

'It's obviously a phobia. She was afraid they'd all come crashing down on her.'

'But we're miles from Edinburgh. Even if they did come crashing down—'

'No, that was while she lived there. It's why she came here. She actually said so.'

The two cousins looked at each other in consternation for some time. Then they both sighed.

'Poor Moira!' said one.

'Yes,' said the other.

'We must be kind to her,' said one.

'Indeed. I don't suppose for a moment it's dangerous.'

From that day on Moira was aware of a constraint in her dealings with the two cousins. Not that they weren't friendly as ever. But there seemed to be something guarded in their attitude, as if they were watching, expecting something . . . Gradually she began to feel that this uneasiness had spread to the rest of the village. People seemed to be watching, waiting.

Moira started avoiding her neighbours, going for even more walks on her own. And more and more frequently did she walk along the low road, talking to her beloved hills.

Several times her conversations were overheard by other villagers, who broadcast the news as soon as they got back to base:

'Talking to herself, she was. Out loud. Like she was holding a real conversation, just like I'm talking to you. Quite gives you the creeps, it does.'

It was when Moira noticed one of the village boys walking past her house, talking loudly to himself, that she began to be suspicious. This happened several times that afternoon. On the last occasion she heard a burst of giggles from behind the hedge. Then the whole flock of youngsters emerged and ran past her house, singing:

> Edinburgh is falling down,
> Falling down, falling down . . .

So Alice had talked. Perhaps Nell too. The whole village knew about her so-called phobias. For a moment she wanted to run in to Nell's and fling reproaches at her. Then she thought better of it and put on her coat instead. She looked round the cottage and remembered that it had never really mattered all that much to her. She had chosen it for the hills, that was all.

She banged the door behind her and set out along the low road.

The evening sun was slanting over the hills; the row to the west was dark-green velvet, outlined against a pale-orange sky; to the east the hills still held the last, tender rays of the sinking sun.

Once she was clear of the houses she paused and spoke to her hills.

'You're beautiful,' she said, 'just beautiful. I could never live without you. You're the best thing my life has ever known.'

Then she started walking briskly, away from the village.

'Come on, then,' she said, 'we're going. I've had enough of that lot. I'm getting out of here, and you're coming with me. Yes, you, every one of you. My beloved hills. And what's more, this time we're not coming back.'

44

The Little Lizard

Ceset spent many hours playing by himself. If you could call it playing, that is. Most of the time he just sat staring ahead. He could hear the other children larking about in the street, but paid no attention. He knew he could join them if he wanted to, and sometimes did. But he found their games noisy, confused, and rather boring. He preferred just sitting in the patio by himself, with his eyes fixed on the high whitewashed wall that bordered their property. He was quite content to have this blank screen in front of him, for his thoughts occupied him well enough.

But the wall also provided entertainment and interest. Mostly there was nothing to see there apart from a deep, wide crack that zigzagged diagonally all the way from top to bottom. And that crack was the source of the action. It might be ants advancing across the wall in formation; it might be a large, long-legged, brightly coloured spider having a look round for any passing prey; or it might be his favourite, the tiny lizard. There were other lizards, of course – a big one, a medium-sized one. Perhaps more than one of each, he just couldn't tell, and it didn't much matter. As for the tiny one, he was persuaded that there was only this one; his little lizard, exquisite and unique.

He spent many hours gazing at it or simply hoping to see it, and thinking about its name. Names, he knew, are terribly important. When one day his father's mother, his *iaia*, called him Peret instead of Ceset he had been deeply offended, and it was a long time before he could think of his *iaia* with the usual warmth. For why did she do a thing like that? It was all very well to say she'd forgotten; forgetting is something you do with things that don't matter – like brushing your teeth or not banging the door. But forgetting *him*, her very own grandson! It was as if she had just rubbed him out of existence.

So names mattered, he knew. Which meant that it was terribly important to get the right one for his lizard. So important that he wondered whether he should ask someone's advice in the matter. But whose? That was the problem. Certainly not his *iaia*. She had shown herself deficient in the business of naming. An inappropriate name might seriously damage the little creature. And he knew not to mention the lizard to his mother, who professed a thorough dislike of all such creepy-crawlies, as she called them. No question of mentioning the matter to his father, who obviously felt a certain impatience, if not outright scorn, for a son of such a retiring disposition. He would have liked Ceset to be like the village boys – noisy, rowdy, enterprising, worrying their parents with the scrapes they got into. The worry with Ceset was that he never got into any scrapes.

No, neither of his parents nor the other boys would be any help at all in the business of naming.

So, day after day and week after week of the hot, dry summer went by, and Ceset still couldn't decide on a name. He would sit in front of the patio wall, willing his pet to come out, singing to it gently in the words of the old Catalan song:

> Sargantana, treu el cap.
> *(Little lizard, just peep out.)*

But his *sargantana* paid no attention, and would sometimes not show its head for days at a time.

Then one day, when the little lizard was sunning itself on the wall, it stayed there motionless for such a long time that Ceset was able to admire every detail: the small, neatly shaped almost triangular head, the slim back tapering into the long, delicate tail, the exquisite dark brown markings running along its whole body, the tiny, claw-like feet.

Ceset moved forward, gently, silently, eager to see more closely, yet afraid to disturb the creature. He stopped a few feet away, close enough to see the gentle bellows movement of its sides as it breathed. He had never had so prolonged and detailed a view of his darling, and was almost overcome with the joy and wonder of the moment.

'*Ets preciosa!*' he whispered. '*Preciosa!*'

The little lizard turned its head slightly in Ceset's direction, in what the boy took to be a nod of acknowledgement. And immediately he knew he'd found the name for his pet. Preciosa, of course!

That moment seemed to go on for ever. The lizard on the wall, the boy a few steps away, aware of an unbreakable bond between them, the sun beating down in the silence of the early afternoon, while all the adults were having their siesta and all the other children had gone off on some noisy foray in a different part of the village.

Sun and silence. Ceset stood so still that he could hear his own heartbeat, and felt sure it was beating in time with the lizard's breath. This was his first experience of eternity. Time had stopped.

From then on Ceset felt even more attached to Preciosa, and spent more hours than ever in the patio, waiting to see his pet, anxious when the tiny creature failed to appear.

He knew the summer was coming to an end. Soon they would all pack their bags and head back to the city. Ceset knew that the chances of seeing a lizard in Barcelona were remote; and anyway, even if one did appear, it wouldn't be Preciosa. He dreaded the thought of going back. So many things he didn't like about life in the city – school, for one thing, where he was herded in with all those other boys, where he was forced to play games, where the streets were full of traffic and strangers, where education's inexorable timetable ruled out any possibility of spending hours by himself, in silence, alone with his own mysterious thoughts. No, what he wanted was an eternal summer, alone in the patio, with Preciosa or at least the hope of seeing Preciosa.

And when Preciosa wasn't available there were other distractions if he tired of his own company. There were the *paletes*, busy on the house next door, which was having an extension built. Ceset wasn't particularly interested in what the jovial gang had to say; but he was fascinated by the bricklayer's art, and would spend ages watching as the workman scooped up a measured quantity of shiny, wet cement, carried it on his trowel over to the growing wall, lifted a brick and skilfully anointed it with the cement. Then came the really exciting moment. With a swift, adroit movement, the brick was turned upside-down and carefully placed on top of the last row. Next the workman tapped with the handle of his trowel along the top of the newly placed brick, to get it to exactly the right level; and then he used the blade of his trowel to scrape off any extra cement, which was then dropped back into the heap on the ground.

But the most wonderful thing of all came at the very end. For then the man would use a very much smaller trowel, to make sure that all the edges were perfectly smooth, all the corners neatly finished off. And this tiny trowel, though the same roughly triangular shape as the big one, was so dainty, and moved so elegantly, that it reminded him of his beloved lizard's head.

He would have liked to tell Jaume, the *paleta*, how much he admired his work, and how his little trowel reminded him of Preciosa. But somehow, although Jaume was friendly and they had even had quite a few little conversations – somehow, Ceset was doubtful about how the workman would take the comparison of his trowel to a lizard. Not everybody, he realized, admired lizards. Some, such as his mother, even hated and feared them. Not that he imagined Jaume was at all likely to fear the harmless creatures. But he might just be one of the people who didn't like them, or even actively disliked them. No, all things considered, he decided not to risk his friendship with the man over the issue. Better to keep the two relationships in separate compartments.

* * *

The summer wore on, till there were only two days to
go. Then the axe would fall, then they would all have to
say goodbye to these rural delights, and join the flood of
other Barcelonese heading back to the city. Ceset felt that
nothing would reconcile him to this misery.

The knowledge of the impending doom had kept him
awake for hours during the night. As a result he slept
much later than usual that morning. He hurried over his
breakfast, aware that the sun had already risen quite high.
Perhaps Preciosa would be out.

As usual he ran to the patio and, as usual, stopped
and advanced quietly and cautiously, not to disturb the
lizard. To his surprise he met Jaume, who was gathering together some of his tools. This was unusual. Jaume
worked for the house next door, not for them.

Jaume finished collecting his things, saw Ceset, and
greeted him.

Ceset returned the greeting and asked him what he was
doing in their patio.

'Your dad asked me to mend the wall here. Look, I've
filled in that great big crack. Looks better, doesn't it?'

Ceset looked at the wall. The huge crack had disappeared.

'But . . . but . . . my lizard – how can it get out?'

'A lizard? Oh, plenty of them about.'

'But, if it can't get out, will it die?'

Jaume shrugged.

'It'll die, won't it?'

Jaume looked at the boy, perplexed. Then he shrugged
again and said:

'I'd better get on with my work next door or I'll get into trouble with the owner. I'm supposed to be working there, not here, you know.'

And he walked away.

Ceset stood in front of the blank wall while the hot tears rose to his eyes. He felt doubly betrayed. By Jaume, whom he had thought of as a friend, and by life itself. Now he would never see Preciosa again. Now he would never know whether his little friend could find its way out again to bask in the glory of the summer sun.

This year, for the first time, he found he could hardly wait to get back to Barcelona, away from the village, away from the hot, sunny, sterile wall.

45

Going back

The woman noticed a yellowish tinge in the narrow channel of sky above her, between the trees on either side of the track. Sulphur, she thought. For some reason, it made her think of sulphur.

Her pace slackened as she advanced. Two more bends, only two more bends and she'd be able to see the cottage. And then only another fifty yards . . .

She was very tired, she ought to be glad her journey was nearly done. She'd be able to rest when she got there, and that was what she needed. Rest.

She realized that her steps had become even slower and heavier. It's this heat, this clammy, oppressive weather, she thought. And the woods. They seem to hold the heat and the damp round you, weighing you down. I'm not used to living among trees any longer, that's what it is.

At last the cottage came into view. The woman noticed the door was open, making the place look almost welcoming. Not for me, though, she thought. It's because of the heat, just the heat. I can hardly expect a welcome. Hardly.

Anyway, she doesn't know.

A few yards from the house she stopped and looked round her. Nothing much changed. Everything a little older, a little shabbier.

Then she picked up her two cases again and advanced.

'I'm back,' she said, standing in the doorway.

The woman sitting by the empty grate looked up – a middle-aged woman in dark, plain clothes. She had grey hair pulled back into a bun, and a lined, weather-beaten face that still preserved its good contours.

She showed no emotion as she gazed at the younger replica of herself standing in the doorway.

'Susan,' she said, and it was more like a statement than a form of address. Then she added:

'I was expecting you.'

'Today?'

'No. Just some day. Anyway, put down those cases and come and sit here. You look tired.'

Susan left the cases near the open door.

'That all your worldly wealth?' asked her mother, as Susan advanced towards the fireplace and sat down opposite her.

'That's it.'

'And what about that man?'

'Barry?'

'Of course. Who else? Have you left him?'

'You could put it that way.'

'Or has he left you?'

'You could put it that way too.' Barry, thought Susan, wasn't important. But I must never let her know that.

'I could have told you that's how it would end,' remarked her mother.

And *I* could have told *you* the very same thing, thought Susan.

Barry was a wanderer by nature, almost by profession. He had turned up one summer and joined the gang of men working in the woods, and life in the quiet little community had suddenly become livelier and more entertaining. All the girls had fallen in love with him – all but Susan, that is.

Barry was wild and good-looking and immensely entertaining. Even the men loved him, and there was always a touch of joy and expectation in the 'Here's Barry!' that announced his arrival in any group. There would be laughter, there would be compliments for the girls and jokes for the men. And always the sheer delight of his dark, confident good looks, his sparkling eyes and the way he had of always making you feel there was something special about you.

'You know about your dad?'

'Yes. I saw it in the paper. What was it?'

'Street accident. Fell in front of a car and died within hours.'

'Drunk?'

'Yes, oh yes. It had to be that. I always knew drink would be the death of him. And yet he was a good man, it was his only fault.'

Susan said nothing.

Outside the stillness had become almost palpable, and the light was fading fast, even though it was only mid-afternoon. Susan felt the oppression even more than before. She looked through the doorway to see the sky, and saw nothing but trees. She got up and walked to the door.

'It's odd, not seeing the sky.'

'It's the trees. You'll get used to it.'

'I ought to. I was brought up here. Only I didn't realize then how much sky there was, so I didn't miss it.'

'There's not that much sky in cities either,' replied her mother. 'Where have you been these three years?'

'In London, mostly.'

'Well then, they haven't got much sky there, have they?'

'More than here. The streets don't crowd in on you the way the trees do.'

Susan stepped outside and looked up. Sky at last, darker now, leaden and threatening. If this is an omen, she thought . . .

'It's so dark,' she said, going back into the room and sitting down.

'There's a storm brewing, that's what it is,' said her mother. 'I'll make a cup of tea.'

Susan felt she ought to offer to help, but she was too tired. Or perhaps too dispirited.

All the same, she was grateful for her mother's unemotional greeting. Not that she expected any histrionics. But when your daughter runs off with a man, doesn't communicate for three years, and then comes back unannounced, six months after her father's death . . .

Well, even Alison Piperson might have been expected to show some emotion, some sort of resentment. But no, she had brought it off in the most casual, unemotional manner. Good for her, thought Susan.

Again she stood up and went over to the door. Looking

up at the sky she found it had turned even blacker, come even closer. And the air was hot and heavy and utterly still. Nothing seemed to be moving – not a leaf, not an insect. All the usual sounds of summer hung in abeyance, waiting.

Susan took a big, gasping breath, as if she couldn't find enough air to fill her lungs. I wish the storm would come, she thought. This one, at least. The other one, the storm inside the house, we may be able to avoid. With Mum's help, of course, only with her help.

Her mother was pouring out the tea when Susan went back in and sat down again.

'Still no sugar?'

'Still no sugar.' Susan took the cup and smiled at her mother.

Her mother looked at her gravely, and nodded.

'Yes,' she said, 'now I'm really beginning to believe you're back.'

Susan sipped her tea, wondering if she would ever manage to let her mother know that she loved her more than anyone else in the world, that she always had. But she could never let her find out, for that would give the show away. And her mother would never recover from the blow.

As they sat drinking their tea in silence the room was illuminated by a flash of lightning.

'Now,' said Alison.

'Now,' said her daughter, and the two women were smiling at each other when the first rumble of thunder was heard.

More lightning and more thunder followed, with the interval between the two getting smaller and smaller.

The distant rumble had now turned to a series of violent crashes.

It was a while before the rain came. At first it arrived in the form of huge, separate drops, landing noisily on the flagstones outside. Then a sudden, fierce eddy of wind brought the rain spattering on the window panes, and through the open doorway, to land on the vinyl of the floor.

'Shall I close the door?' asked Susan, beginning to get up.

'No, leave it for the moment. It's so welcome. We can mop up later.'

Soon the wind died down, and the rain fell straight, heavy, determined, forming puddles outside the door, with only a few splashes now getting into the house.

She said it was so welcome, thought Susan. Am I welcome too? Shall I ever know?

She thought of the misery that had clouded her last few years before leaving home, and which had forced her to go off with Barry.

Barry had taken a lot of persuading. For once in his life, so he said, he was perfectly happy where he was, and didn't feel like moving just yet. Barry was a free agent, he could come and go as he liked, he could have walked off with more or less any of the girls in the neighbourhood. He didn't even need to walk off with any of them, anyway. They were all perfectly happy to take him, or rather, let him take them, on any terms. So what was the point of saddling himself with one of them, especially now, when, for once in his life he felt like staying?

The one thing she knew about Barry with absolute

certainty was that he was utterly incapable of keeping a secret. And so she couldn't tell him her real reason for wishing to leave. She had to pretend a love she simply didn't feel. Not that she wasn't attracted to him. And if he had come wooing her in the conventional manner, with an engagement ring and the promise of marriage, she would have been only too delighted to accept him and fall in love accordingly.

But there had been no question of that. Barry liked her, flirted with her, as with all the other girls. But all he wanted was an easy lay, with no strings attached. In the end what made him decide to follow her suggestion was a rather unpleasant encounter with the irate father of one of his many sweethearts, a girl who had discovered she was pregnant and insisted that Barry was responsible. Barry had taken the matter rather lightly at first, pointing out that even if it could be proved he had been the girl's lover, it could certainly not be proved he was the only one. The offended father had reacted violently, and had threatened even further violence.

At this point Barry, who disliked what he called 'complications', had suddenly seen the attractions of Susan's plan.

'Dear Mum,' she had written, 'I love Barry and I'm going off with him. I know this is the only way, so don't worry over me. I love you too, and I always will.'

She hoped her omission of any mention of her father would not be seen as significant.

The first few months with Barry had been quite happy. Susan missed her mother, but was so thankful to have escaped from the problems at home that she turned a blind eye to all the unsatisfactory aspects of her present situation. And their itinerant life, full of the unexpected, had seemed rather charming at first. Then the novelty had worn off for both of them. Barry had felt tied in the end, and had not hesitated to tell her so.

'I've never been bound, and I never will be. That's why I've led this wandering, unprofitable life. I've given up security, prosperity, all the things other men value most, for the sake of my freedom. And I'm not prepared to give that up, not for you and not for anyone or anything.'

After making a similar statement on several occasions, Barry disappeared one morning, and she never heard of him again. She drifted to London and lived on odd jobs and Income Support. She hated the life, but could think of nothing else to do. Not go home, at any rate, that was out of the question.

It was while she was reading the papers in the public library, one wet afternoon when she had drifted in for shelter in the middle of a job-hunting session, that she saw the name Piperson in the Births, Marriages and Deaths columns.

So she could go back now. She knew her mother would be broken-hearted over her husband's death, and would be glad of the comfort of even an errant daughter. What held her back was the fear that she would be unable to conceal her resentment towards the dead man. Whatever happens, she told herself, I must never let her guess the truth. She's immensely strong, but that would break her.

So she had spent six months schooling herself, trying to see herself holding an easy conversation with her mother, talking in a normal, loving way about her dead father. She soon realized she could never hope to do this convincingly unless she had first managed to banish some of the resentment from her heart. So she had spent the months working on this, trying to blot out her later memories, trying to recapture the love and admiration she had felt for her father as a child, before he had destroyed it all.

'Now, look here, Susan, there's no need to make all this fuss. I've done the decent thing by you, waited till you were grown up. Not every father would.'

She seethed with anger at his self-righteous tone. Later on, as information about more and more scandals was meted out to an eager public, she came to realize that his abstinence till she was sixteen was perhaps a matter of caution rather than consideration for her feelings. But at first she had known nothing. The inconceivable seemed to be happening to her, and she had felt trapped, disgusted, horrified, and immensely guilty.

From the start she had realized that she had nowhere to turn to, for her mother idolized her husband, while regretting his tendency to drink too much, which she considered the only fault in an otherwise exemplary character.

The girl felt too guilty and ashamed to turn to anyone else; and, besides, if anything was to be done to help her, there was no way of preventing her mother from finding out. And if Alison Piperson had not managed to retain the unconditional love of her husband, she had certainly won it from her daughter. Even at sixteen Susan had been convinced that the revelation of her father's misdeeds would completely shatter her mother. And how could she do this to the very being she loved most on this earth?

In the end she had taken the only path that seemed open to her.

For a long time the sound of the rain and the now slowly retreating thunder seemed a pleasant and perfectly adequate substitute for conversation. Gradually the light returned, the thunder died away, and the rain stopped.

Alison stood up and went over to the door.

'Come,' she said, 'it's a different world now.'

Susan got up and stood beside her mother in the open doorway. The oppressive heaviness had completely vanished. Instead, a light breeze was swaying the branches in a fresh, green, wet world.

'We needed that,' said the older woman.

'Yes,' agreed her daughter, 'it's lovely now.' She took a deep breath, enjoying the acrid smell of the wet earth after the long drought. 'Smells good, doesn't it?'

Her mother didn't answer. She was staring ahead with a preoccupied expression on her face. They stood there in silence, side by side, breathing in the fresh, sweet air.

After a while Alison spoke.

'I told a lie earlier on,' she admitted. 'I said drink was your father's only fault. But there's not many of us, even among the best, with only one fault. He had another. Only one, but it was a bad one. He told me after you'd gone.'

Susan stood beside her mother, feeling no need for words. The only sound to break the silence was the now erratic dripping of the last of the rain as it slid off the shining, refreshed leaves.

46

The Numbers Game

It took me a while to realize what was happening. At first I just seemed to be dialling more wrong numbers than usual. Carelessness, I supposed.

Some people were quite snappish about it, as if it was my fault. After getting the same man five times running he suggested – politely, I have to admit – that perhaps the exchange could help me.

It did, and I got through all right.

And that, you see, is what kept me from realizing just how odd it all was. For, if the exchange could get the number for me, it must simply be that I was making a mistake in the dialling. Or so it seemed.

And there was another thing that kept me from seeing what was happening – many of the numbers gave me no trouble at all.

All the same, it kept on happening, no matter how carefully I dialled. I puzzled over it for weeks, till one day I decided I must try to crack this riddle, and I wrote down all the numbers that were giving me trouble. I spent a long time looking at them, to see what they had in common. I did all sorts of interesting mathematical things with them – factorization, equations, progressions of the arithmetic, geometric and harmonic varieties, but got nowhere.

Then I wrote down all the ones I dialled regularly without any problems.

And that was what gave me my clue. For I noticed that none of them had a 4 or a 5 in them. And then I looked at the others, the bad ones, and saw they all had either a 4 or a 5 in them, and some had both.

This, I felt, was quite a breakthrough, though I couldn't see how I could put it to any practical use, short of persuading all the friends in question to have their phone number changed. I imagined a conversation with, say, Hector, to that effect.

'By the way, Hector, I wonder if you'd do me a favour.'

'Anything to help a friend. What can I do for you?'

'Well, I was wondering if you wouldn't mind changing your phone number.'

Hector looks at me in surprise.

'What on earth for?'

'This is the tricky bit. I know it sounds odd, but I'm having difficulty dialling your present number.'

'Difficulty? What do you mean, difficulty? You mean you find it hard to remember?'

'No, not that.'

'Because all you have to do', he goes on, ignoring my disclaimer, 'is consult your address book. Or feed the number into your telephone memory, then you'll only have one digit to dial.'

'But it isn't that, I tell you. I can remember your number perfectly well – 655157.'

'Well then, what's the problem?'

'Just that I get someone else every time I dial that number.'

'Not *every* time. You got through to me all right this morning.'

'Yes, but I had to ask the exchange. I'd already tried several times, and I always got this hysterical woman swearing at me.'

That's what it would be like, I know. And though Hector is a reasonable sort of a fellow, and would understand about not wanting to get through to the hysterical woman again, still, I'm sure he'd refuse to consider having his number changed.

In the end I decided to enlist his help with the actual problem, asking him to check that I was dialling correctly. He thought it was all a bit queer, but agreed to watch me as I dialled our mutual friend Morag.

He was standing beside me, so he heard the voice at the other end of the line. A man's voice. Hector was none too pleased about that, I can tell you. He rather fancies Morag.

'Don't worry,' I reassured him. 'Just you try dialling this time.'

So he dialled and got through to Morag, as I knew he would. Then he had a bit of a problem explaining why he'd rung her. Telling her about *my* problem, I mean. She obviously thought we were both mad.

My next breakthrough came when I tried ringing my mother. Her number ends in 5, so I knew I'd probably get someone else. Perhaps because I was thinking of this, and wondering why I hadn't tried getting it through the exchange, I pressed the wrong button – actually saw myself doing it. Instead of the final 5, I pressed a 4. And a moment later there was Mum's voice at the of the line!

I was so astonished that I exclaimed, 'Is that actually *you*, Mum?' This seemed to surprise her somewhat.

'Of course it's me. Who do you expect to hear when you dial my number? The Queen?'

'But I dialled the wrong number!'

I was so excited about my discovery that I really couldn't think of anything else to say to her. She was clearly puzzled by the whole episode.

I've cracked the code! I thought. 4 and 5 have changed places, I bet that's what it is. So I set about phoning lots of people in the trouble zone, just reversing 4 and 5, and it worked like a charm. By the time I'd finished I'd run out of small talk, and I think a lot of my friends were left wondering why on earth I had phoned when I had nothing to say.

For I'm not telling too many people about this strange experience I'm going through. After all, you never know. They might think there was something – you know – sort of queer about me. And it's not me, it's the numbers.

Anyway, the great thing was that I'd cracked the code, I could now use the phone like any normal human being, provided I remembered to reverse those two numbers.

And that would have been that, if it hadn't been for Hector. My fatal mistake had been letting him know anything about it. Next time we met he asked me how I was getting on with my dialling problem.

'Fine, fine,' I said. 'I've cracked it.'

I wanted to leave it at that, but he insisted. Said he'd been thinking a lot about it, and that it really did seem an extraordinary business.

I was all for playing down the matter.

'It was quite simple, really, once I'd examined the facts carefully.' Again I tried to drop the subject.

But Hector's got a bit of the terrier in him. Won't let go, when he gets hold of something.

Grudgingly, I had to admit the truth.

'It's just that 4 and 5 have changed places, that's all,' I said casually, trying to make it sound as ordinary and everyday as possible.

It didn't work, of course. Not with Hector. He just about hit the ceiling. He's got one of those rather literal, factually oriented minds that thinks everything's verifiable. No sense of wonder, that's what's wrong with Hector.

What amazes me, and always has, is the predictability of the material world. I think it's something most people would agree about – that it's predictable, I mean, not that this is amazing. But I think it's absolutely unbelievable. After all, why should things always behave in the same way? Once you start thinking about it you see that it's utterly astonishing.

For instance: I let go the book I'm holding in my hand, and it falls – always and inevitably downwards. I drop this glass I've just picked up, and it too falls – downwards, like the book, the only difference being that the glass shatters into fragments. And it never seems to strike anybody that it's odd that the book doesn't shatter into fragments too. Or that one of them doesn't fall upwards instead, if only for the sake of variety.

So, you see, to anybody who's in the habit of meditating on this sort of thing, this little trick the numbers are playing on me isn't all that amazing. I'd have been perfectly content to leave it at that. It's not all that difficult to dial 4 instead of 5 and 5 instead of 4, once you get used to it.

Of course, I *would* like to know why it's happening, and I have to admit I've not got the faintest idea. And I'd like to think it's not going any further. It would be no fun having to dial 7842518 every time you needed a 6, for instance. And the question arises, would our over-burdened telephone system be able to cope with so many digits?

Anyway, this is pure speculation. I've no reason whatever to assume the numbers would want to play that sort of trick on me. After all, I think I've taken this 4 and 5 business quite well, and I hope they'll take that into consideration. I'm not worried, really.

No, it's my friends who are the real problem. Won't leave the matter alone – thanks to Hector, need I say? Felt it was too much of a responsibility to keep the matter to himself. So I keep getting tender enquiries after my health, worried looks, subtle (!) hints about doctors. I've even heard the word 'shrink' mentioned. Casually, of course, oh, ever so casually!

Had quite a set-to with Morag this morning, inches deep in concern for me. Simply couldn't get her to see that the problem was with the numbers, not me.

'Look!' I said, with just the tiniest touch of exasperation in my voice, 'you've heard of computer viruses, haven't you?'

'No,' she said, 'I haven't.' She sounded distinctly unreceptive.

That rather destroyed my argument. I was about to establish a perfectly valid parallel. But, faced with such monumental ignorance, what can you do?

I tried again.

'It's something like Fuzzy Logic,' I said.

Morag's eyes opened very, very wide.

'*Fuzzy* logic, you said?'

'That's right. There's this American guy—'

'But we're not talking about logic, are we? We're talking about numbers.'

'Right! So we're talking about numbers. Fuzzy numbers, if you like. You understand the concept, do you?'

'No, not really.' Morag didn't look at all happy. I could see she was backing away – mentally, I mean. 'In fact,' she went on, 'I don't really understand much about numbers at all, except that four comes before five, and not the other way round.' Nervously, almost apologetically, she added, 'I'm really much happier with words than numbers.'

'All right,' I said, patient to the end. 'I'll give you it in words. Listen. *Ya ya woochi, yarago woochi tumpa, tumpa yarago wah.* Does that make sense?'

'Yes,' she quavered, moving unobtrusively towards the door. 'Yes, that makes perfect sense. Of course.'

I let her go. What, after all, was the point of arguing with someone who thought she could see anything in that improvised piece of nonsense? I've no doubt someone else will see the state she's in mentally and have her properly looked after. Poor Morag!

Ironic to think it was she who used the word 'shrink'.

47

And still the cars go past

It's good, sitting in the doorway, watching the cars sliding past, noiselessly, effortlessly. Swsssh, swsssh . . . Very soothing, very peaceful.

Other people complain – too many cars, you take your life in your hands every time you cross the road, the place is full of foreigners, what's happened to our quiet little fishing village?

But then, this is what you get, if your quiet little fishing village is on the main road between Barcelona and the French frontier. And yes, of course, it can be a bit of a nuisance at times. Still, when you've got all your housework finished, you've been to the market and put everything away into the fridge, and cooked and eaten your meal, and washed up, it's nice to sit at the open door, watching the world go by in the big, powerful cars.

It was fishing boats, not cars, that we looked out to, when I was a girl. You crossed the road and the railway line and there you were on the shore, with the sand easing its way into your *espardenyes*, and the boats, the beautiful fishing boats pulled up onto the beach, and the fishermen busy with their nets . . .

The boats, with their lovely names – *Encarna, Estrella del Mar, Filomena* . . . And the men there, all the strongest, bravest, liveliest young men of the village, cleaning out the boats, getting them ready to go out to sea again in late evening. And at night you saw their lights in a splendid half-circle right across the great bay. The lights and their reflection, all dancing and shining and wavering, so sometimes you couldn't tell which was lantern and which reflection. And you thought about the nets full of shimmering fish, writhing about, catching the light with their polished scales, sending sparks of light out over the sea.

Beautiful, beautiful . . .

Yes, I see why my generation complains. All that's gone. But it's not the cars and the tourists and the *veraneantes* spilling out from Barcelona every summer to enjoy the bathing and the cool sea breezes. That's not what put an end to the fishing. All that was dying anyway, with all the lorries bringing fish in from the furthest places – Scotland, even.

And all these people here, these crowds everybody complains about, they've filled the gap.

So I don't mind the swsssh-swsssh of their cars. I don't mind the crowded pavements, and the queues at the market stalls. It all serves to drive away the emptiness.

I fell into a great, black empty hole the morning we heard the *Filomena* had gone down. And I had to hide my grief, my own, private grief. Of course we were all shocked and saddened by the loss. They were our men, every one of them. And the wives and the mothers and the sweethearts

of the drowned men were all taken to the heart of the
village, supported, pitied, comforted . . .

And I was left out, for no one knew I was in love with
Esteve. Not even Esteve himself.

Why were we taught to be like that? So secret, so
hidden, so shackled by lies and half-truths and decep-
tions? Why could I not have told him? Just because he
didn't speak first? It would have been wrong, immodest,
indecent; that's what we were taught to believe. And I
see these young people of today living by different rules,
more open, more honest. Why were we not allowed to
be like that in our time? Why did we have to sit in the
doorway working at our pillow lace, pretending we didn't
even see the handsome young men walking past?

Suppose I had had the courage to tell Esteve, would the
skies have fallen down?

Would the sea have dried up and would all the fish
have perished? And if he had rejected me I should have
been filled with shame and misery, but still, I should
at least have spoken the supreme words – I love you.
Words that Esteve's death deprived me for evermore of
speaking. For I knew then, knew it long before his death,
that I should never love another man.

That last day, his last day, was the first time he looked
at me – really looked at me, I mean. Of course he had seen
me hundreds of times, for we were brought up in the same
village, and in those days everybody knew everybody else.
And he had seen me, seen this girl called Carola nearly
every day of his life. But there's a way of seeing that
is really a way of not seeing, and that's what most of us
do nearly all the time. Seeing the outside only. And that
wasn't the way I saw him.

Oh, I saw the outside, all right. Saw the hard muscles and the taut, tanned skin; saw the slender waist and the wide chest with the dark hair showing through his open shirt. Saw the handsome face with its dark, shining eyes. Yes, I saw him all right, on the outside, and I won't say that wasn't part of the attraction.

But not all, for I saw him on the inside too. Saw the meaning of his slow smile, understood the gentleness in his manner, the thoughtful look in his eyes. I could see that deep down he was a good man. And there was something more.

There was something inside him that was saying to me, this is your man.

So I sit here and think about the past that never was, and I let the swsssh of the cars lull my sorrow and my senses, and I drift into a different, less tragic world . . .

'*Bona tarda*, Carola.'

I start up.

'*Bona tarda*, Mundeta. How are you?'

'Well, still living. That's the best one can say. Some of us have sorrows that can't be forgotten,' Mundeta sighs.

I agree with her; but at the same time I also think of the other women whose lives were ruined when the *Filo* went down, and many others too in the fishing community, who have somehow managed to get their lives together again. Mundeta's case is as sad as theirs, for she was engaged to be married to Quimet; but she hasn't allowed herself to get over it. It's the subject of all her conversation, the very substance of her life.

'Just two days before the wedding.'

How often has she said these words?

'Two days, and when we parted Quimet said, "This is the last time I go out with the boats." For he'd decided to give up fishing and had got a job in one of the market gardeners' places, just to keep me from worrying every night when the boats were out.'

And *I* think, my loss is even greater, for I lost the whole of my love. I wasn't even left with a memory. Just a hope, a new, vibrant hope.

For that day, the last day of his life, Esteve saw me. Yes, he really saw me for the first time.

I was sitting at the door, shelling peas for the supper, and Esteve and his father passed, with the usual greeting.

'*Bona tarda*, Carola.'

'*Bona tarda tinguin*,' I replied.

As he passed, Esteve looked at me. And for once it wasn't just the polite passing glance. For a moment his eyes held mine, and I knew something was happening. Then he walked on; but turned back at once and I could see he was going to say something. Just then his father called him, telling him to hurry up. Esteve obeyed. But as he was turning to go he spoke:

'*Fins demà*, Carola.'

'*Fins demà*, Esteve.'

Till tomorrow, I thought, and my heart was bursting inside me. How could I wait till the next day? For I knew it had happened at last. I knew that the next day I would receive his new love, and enfold it in my long, patient love.

For a long time I sat in a dream, till my mother came and scolded me for not getting on with my work.

'It's so hot,' I said. 'It's too hot to work.'

'But it's not too hot to eat. Get a move on, or supper

will be late, and you know what your father will say.'

And it was hot, terribly, frighteningly hot. The air seemed on fire. And as the evening advanced it grew hotter still.

We knew there was going to be a storm. But the men went out to sea all the same. They couldn't afford to lose their catch, and, besides, you never know where the storm's going to break.

It broke over the village. At midnight we were all wakened by the loudest crash of thunder anyone had ever heard. We all gathered downstairs in the dining room, with Grandmother in her rocking chair, telling the beads of her rosary and praying for salvation. When at last the storm had moved off she insisted that it was through the direct intervention of the Holy Virgin, who had heard her prayers. We went back to bed, but not to sleep, for we knew the storm had moved out to sea.

Next morning came the news that the *Filomena* had gone down with all her crew.

Grandmother didn't seem to take it in. She kept on repeating that we'd been saved because of the way she had prayed to the Virgin Mary to save us.

I could stand it no longer, and snapped back:

'You'd have been better to pray for the *Filomena* instead. We were on dry land, after all. No fear of us drowning.'

And in my mind I added, More's the pity. For I didn't want to go on living, not without Esteve, not now I was sure he cared.

* * *

So I sit in the doorway watching the cars flit past, and I listen to Mundeta's eternal complaint; and the swsssh-swsssh of the cars flows over her lament and over my own silent sorrow for my lost dream, lulling the pain, lulling it, till dream and loss merge into a gentle, accepting reverie.

And still the cars go past, taking my pain with them.

48

Earthquake

They had been warned, of course. But then, they had already been warned so many times about this great disaster. Sometimes it was the scientists in their white coats, sometimes the old people who studied the movement of the birds and the insects – the ants are all fleeing! – sometimes the priest who told them that the wrath of God was really going to explode this time. And so it went on. If you listened to them all you'd never have a moment's peace.

An earthquake was the last thing Lucas was thinking of as he went to empty his basket onto the pile of carob pods at the back of the cave. Holding the heavy basket by its two handles, carrying it in front of him, he looked down with satisfaction at the dark, gleaming pods. It had been a good harvest, it would help to see the mule through the winter.

Near the entrance the cave was high enough for him to stand up in; at the back, four paces further into the side of the hill, he had to walk with his head bowed, to avoid hitting it against the rough, gravel roof.

Just as he leaned forward to empty his basket he felt

he was losing his balance. Had the ground under his feet moved? Nonsense, he just wasn't concentrating on what he was doing. He tipped the basket over, and as he did so he was surprised at the volume of sound apparently produced by the carob pods as they cascaded down the darkly shining pile at the far end of the cave.

The sound grew, louder and louder, and continued long after his basket had been emptied. Then the hard-packed earth under his feet shook again, a great crashing, rumbling sound filled the cave, and he was thrown to the ground.

The whole world had turned to dust and darkness. Nearly choking, drawing his limbs free from the shower of stones that had landed on him, Lucas managed to struggle into a sitting position. He was bruised and deafened and struggling for breath, but not seriously hurt.

His first reaction was sheer astonishment. So they had all been right, the men in their white coats, and the muttering old women, even the priest himself! The long-foretold earthquake had struck at last.

With his handkerchief held to his mouth he waited for the dust to subside. Then, as breathing became easier, he looked round in all directions, hoping to find a ray of light that would give him some sense of direction. But the darkness was total, impenetrable.

If only he had some idea of which way he was facing he would try to shift the stones and rubble and clear a way out of the cave. But he had been thrown down with such violence that he had lost all sense of direction; and there was no point in trying to clear a path for himself if he was facing the wrong way. He might end up trying to burrow his way right through the mountain!

Then it occurred to him that he could tell which way he was facing if he could find the heap of carob pods.

Stones, rubble, gravel – there seemed to be nothing else round about him. At last his fingers alighted on something long and smooth, and less hard. Just to make sure he lifted the object to his face and sniffed at it. Yes, there was the sweet, musty smell of carob. He felt he had never smelled anything so delectable in his life.

But one single carob pod was not an infallible indicator. The force of the rock fall might well have scattered the whole heap. Feeling about, he came across another pod, and then another. Then a whole pile of them buried under rubble.

Now he knew which way he was facing. With difficulty, for he had little space to move in, he edged himself gradually round till he was facing the exit, and started moving the rocks and rubble in front of him.

The first problem was to find space to put all the displaced material. He soon realized the only thing to do was to lay everything behind him, packing it with extreme care so that it would not take up any more space than he had cleared with each stone, each handful of rubble. The free space round about him was infinitely less than the space occupied by the rubble between him and the open air, supposing the exit was blocked all the way to the track outside. There might be many hours of work ahead of him.

Slowly and cautiously, he lifted stone after stone, handfuls of rubble, and packed them all carefully behind him.

And then he came across the second problem. For, as he tugged at a large stone in his path, there was a sudden rattle of smaller stones, more dust, and then another fall of rock right in front of him, driving him back against the pile of stuff he had moved, right up against the inside wall of the cave.

Alarmed, he remained very still, in an awkward crouching position, not daring to move. There was now even less space round about him than there had been at first. Now he saw there was no point in knowing which way the entrance to the cave lay, for he dare not try moving as much as another stone, without the danger of precipitating a major fall.

Moving with infinite care he managed to get into a sitting position, with his back against the pile of stones and rubble he had shifted.

So that was it, he thought. Nothing he could do except wait for help. No point in exhausting himself by calling out. There would be nobody to hear.

The more he thought about it, the less likely it seemed that help would come quickly. His house lay half a mile from the village, and, now that his wife was dead and the two boys had found work in the city, he lived alone. Even if the villagers knew about the earthquake and sent someone to see if he was all right, they would have no idea where to look for him. Finding the house empty, they might just assume he had gone off to the town for the day.

And, anyway, perhaps the village had been affected, or even the whole district. He thought of the terrible earthquake that had destroyed ten villages in Iran, and once again he remembered part of the television report he had seen in the local café a few days before. Once again he was looking at the picture he had tried to erase from his consciousness – a field covered with men, women and

children, all lying motionless on the ground. In the foreground, an old man, sitting on the bare earth beside two
children – dead? seriously wounded? The man was looking at them, mechanically wiping the tears from his face
with the corner of his loose garment. That was the only
movement in the whole scene – the hand rising every few
seconds to wipe the flowing tears, with a field of bodies
lying very still in the background.

Now this memory suggested a vision of his own village
in ruins, with the football pitch covered by the corpses of
all his relatives, his friends, his neighbours. Thank God the
boys were away, safe in the city, many miles from here.
Thank God, he thought for the first time, that Encarna was
dead. She would at least be spared the desolation.

As for him, there was nothing he could do. His sense
of powerlessness left him stunned at first. Was this, then,
to be the end of his life? Just to sit here in the dark, till he
died of lack of oxygen, of hunger and thirst? Or perhaps
there might be a fresh fall of rock that would kill him
outright.

Yes, that would no doubt be the better option, if he
was not to be rescued. At least it would be quicker. Better
than sitting here for endless hours, days even, powerless
to help himself.

As he adjusted to the situation he began to feel less
stunned and helpless. There was nothing he could do to
remedy his physical plight. But what about his mind and
his feelings? If he had only a few more hours to live,
perhaps a few more days, how was he going to spend the
time? The choice was entirely up to him, after all. For once
he could do nothing – *had* to do nothing – with a perfectly
clear conscience. No need to feel guilty about that field he

ought to be hoeing, or that crack in the kitchen wall that was letting in the rain, or that pile of junk in the attic that he ought to get rid of, or the lock on the front door that might just work for another few months if he gave it a good oiling, if only he could get round to tackling it.

Since Encarna's death he'd really rather let things slide. It was different when she was there, she was always so careful about everything, she took such a pride in their little house.

The first few months of their marriage had been spent with her parents – old Cornelio, drunk most days, and his wife, Prudencia, nagging all the time. And then, that glorious day when they had carted all their belongings out to the little house outside the village, and set up on their own!

Why am I thinking of this now? he asked himself. I may be dead in a few hours or a few days, perhaps even in less than a minute, if there's another tremor. And then he wondered what he really ought to be thinking of in such a situation.

Seeing Encarna dying of cancer had made him intensely aware of the certainty of death, and how this ordeal could be faced. He thought of the dignity and resignation his wife had shown, and how impressed he had been by her effort to live life to the full right to the end. That's the way it ought to be, he thought. I don't want to be fuming and fretting, wondering if I'll ever get out of here, straining my ears for the sound of salvation . . .

The word 'salvation' prompted a different train of thought. I could be praying, he thought, I *should* be praying, if what the priest says is right. Praying for help or praying for forgiveness. Praying for all the people in the village, who may be even worse off than I am. He tried to pray for them all, but found it difficult, not knowing how urgent their need of his prayers might be. Perhaps, after all, it was they who should be praying for him. At least there could be no doubt as to how bad his situation was.

His thoughts were interrupted by a very slight sound inside the cave. Listening carefully, he came to the conclusion that it must be either a large insect – a beetle, perhaps? – or one of those tiny lizards that darted so lightly in and out of the cracks in the hot, sun-baked walls. A great wave of concern, even love, for this frail creature surged through him. He thought of all the hundreds, even thousands, of small beings that the earthquake must have killed or injured.

His thoughts drifted off, back to that day he had brought Encarna to their own house for the first time. Since her death he had been unable to think of their shared happiness without sorrow. All his thoughts of her had been clouded by the memory of her illness and her imminent death, and with his fear of being left alone. But now the thought of her brought delight.

Another tiny sound reminded him that he was not alone in the cave, and he felt a sense of companionship with the small, unknown creature that was trying to get on with its life in this dark, restricted space. Might it perhaps find its way out to fresh air and a clear sky above? And would he ever find *his* way out?

A wave of despair overcame him. What chance was there that he would ever be rescued?

I have no future. The words sounded as clearly in his mind as if he had heard them spoken. No future, and very little in the way of present either. But he had the past.

As he sat huddled in what was left of the cave, Lucas gave himself over completely to reliving the past.

That, surely, was the best he could do with what little time might be left to him. He was going to go over all the happy moments, savouring them all. It would be like having two lives – the one he had lived almost unconsciously, just because it was there, and the one he chose to relive, made up of hope and happiness. And he wasn't going to follow any strict chronological order. He was going to let his mind drift, rejecting the bad bits, relishing the good bits. If he must die, then he would die saturated by happy memories.

Encarna was with him. They were walking together along the dusty road from the village, on their way to their new home. In front of them the mule drawing the cart, which was filled with all their personal belongings – a bed and the bedclothes, a table, three assorted chairs, a few pots and pans, some crockery, a little cutlery, and their Sunday clothes. That was about it. They were so happy, constantly turning to look at each other, exchanging smiles, holding hands, laughing in anticipation of the delights of having a place of their own.

That was yesterday, thirty years ago, today. It's still here, inside me, every bit as real as any of the more recent images I can conjure up. What I did this very morning, a few hours ago, is as far beyond recovery as that walk behind the cart that was carrying our whole world for us.

Encarna, after she had learned that her cancer was inoperable. The grey look on her face, its lines suddenly deepened, the sense of strain and suffering. And then the smile that had lit up her features as she turned to him and said, 'Never mind, Lucas. We'll have a few more months yet. A few months is a very long time.'

They had done a lot of living in those few months. A lot of living and a lot of dying too. For Encarna had learned how to die, and, watching her, he too had learned.

'I'm glad the boys are both away,' she had said one day. 'It means we have more time with each other.' Knowing how she adored her two sons, Lucas had been almost awed by the thought of what this revealed of her love for him.

The hours passed, and Lucas began to feel hungry. He picked up one of the carob pods, dusted it carefully with his handkerchief, and bit into it. Being freshly gathered, its flesh was moist, almost juicy. He hadn't bitten into a carob pod for years. We're spoiled now, he thought. We all have so much of everything . . . who would bother about a carob pod nowadays? Fodder, that's all we think it is.

He was at the top of one of the hills that surrounded the village, with his arm round the trunk of the twisted tree that grew on the summit. He was panting, and his two brothers were still labouring up the slope.

'It's not fair, you're bigger, it's not fair, of course you win every time!' they were complaining.

As the two younger boys reached the top and flung themselves on the ground Lucas laughed and, to confirm his superiority, climbed nimbly up the tree.

Still laughing, he flung a few carob pods down to them.

'There you are, don't say I'm not good to you.'

He picked one for himself, the best and richest and fullest he could find, and bit into it.

Forty years later the sweetness of that first bite merged with the sweetness of the pod he had just bitten into. He was crouching in the darkness of the cave, he was sitting on the branch of that carob tree, his legs dangling, the breeze blowing in his hair. In front of him stretched the dry, dusty little fields sloping down to the village, with all the houses huddled together. He could make out his own street, with his house at the near end. He watched as the figure of a woman came out and stood, looking round. Then she raised one hand to her mouth and Lucas knew she was calling her sons. But the rustle of the breeze in the leaves of the tree made it impossible to hear her voice at that distance.

'Look,' he said to his brothers, 'she's calling us. But we can't hear her, can we?'

They all agreed they couldn't hear her, and, with great hilarity, they decided they were therefore entitled to stay where they were. She could call, but they wouldn't go. He could still feel the great surge of freedom that this defiance had brought.

Reliving that sense of freedom, he drifted off into sleep.

It wasn't till the afternoon of the second day that they set off to look for him. The earthquake had caused so much damage in the village, with many houses destroyed and a number of people trapped in the rubble, that no one had had time to think of finding out whether Lucas was all right in his lonely house half a mile along the little track that led nowhere.

At first they couldn't understand where he had got to. Then they remembered about the cave where he kept his carob harvest, saw what had happened, and realized Lucas must be trapped inside.

They had to work very slowly and carefully, for fear of a further landslide.

'Lucas!' they kept on calling, 'Lucas!'

His mother was calling him, but he wasn't going to answer. As long as he couldn't actually hear her he was entitled to stay where he was, swinging in the branches of the tree up on top of the hill. This was life, this was freedom!

Lucas! Lucas!

When at last they got to him he was weak and dazed. They laid him in the shade and revived him with water, then a little wine. And they told him about all the damage the earthquake had done in the village.

'You're lucky,' they told him, 'your house is all right.'

They helped him to get up and walk unsteadily over to the house. A little damage had been done, but nothing serious.

They left him, advising him to go to bed and have a good sleep.

'You'll be right as rain by tomorrow,' they said.

But he didn't go to bed. Instead he wandered around disconsolately. He felt he had been robbed. Robbed of Encarna, robbed of his youth and his happiness. Robbed, in a way, of his own death. For he realized that, following Encarna's example, he had been able to make a relatively good job of facing extinction. Would he do as well a second time?

In the cave he had been given back his childhood, with its indomitable sense of power and hope and independence; he had been given back the happiness and the sorrow of his years with Encarna. And now, once again, he was alone.

Then he thought of his small, unidentified companion in the cave, and wondered whether it had managed to get out. Slowly, still feeling shaken, he walked across and stood in front of the remains of his prison. For a while he saw no movement. Then, from behind one of the large stones at his feet, a small, shapely head appeared, and remained very still for a few moments. Reassured, the tiny lizard drew itself up onto the rock and lay there in the sun, its sides gently moving in and out, like a pair of delicate bellows.

There are hundreds and thousands of the creatures all over the place, Lucas told himself. Why should I assume that this is the one that was in the cave with me? I don't even know whether it was a lizard. Might have been one of those large beetles, perhaps even a snake. And yet, he couldn't help feeling relieved at the sight of this lizard sunning itself on the rock.

I'll never know, of course, he thought. That's the trouble with daily life, as you live it. The life he had lived – chosen to live – in the cave had been different, with its sense of total conviction.

With a sigh he turned and went back to the house. He supposed he ought to find something to do.

He stood in the doorway, gazing abstractedly at the new outline the hill had acquired, at the remains of his cave. And then he walked into the kitchen, feeling lost and purposeless, still longing to get back into the past he had recovered during his recent captivity.

The kitchen was the only part of the house to have been affected by the earthquake. He noticed a little heap of plaster lying on the floor near the back door, and saw that the crack in the wall was now so wide that he could see right through it.

Instead of feeling annoyance or dismay he felt relief. Now he was truly back in the present, released from the obsession of his journey into the past. There was a job to be done.

With a returning sense of purpose and reality, he went out to the shed where he kept the bag of cement.

49

Always the sea

'Can I keep it?'

'Yes, of course. It's only a stone.'

And a stone, I knew, was a bit of solidified earth. And this stone was now mine. That made me a landowner, didn't it? In a small way, the smallest possible way; but a landowner all the same.

The man was looking out to sea, not noticing me any more, obviously thinking about something else. And all I could think of was the stone. My stone. Does he know he's just given away a bit of his property? I wondered.

Still staring out to sea, the man spoke again.

'It's a bugger,' he said.

'What's a bugger?'

The man turned round, looking surprised. I decided he must have forgotten all about me.

'Oh, the sea,' he said. 'Always the sea. You just can't trust it. Not with anything. Not with anyone.'

I said:

'I don't want to trust it. I prefer the land.' And my fingers closed tight round my stone.

'So you don't want to go to sea?'

I shook my head.

'That's good,' said the man. 'Tell your father. Tell him you'll never go to sea.'

'My father? Why should I tell him that?'

The man didn't answer.

I was looking at the ground, seeing more stones. They were none of them quite as good as my one. But then, mine was special – big enough to fill my whole hand, smooth, shiny greyish white, with little sparkly bits. Quartz, I learned later. The other stones weren't like that, but they were quite good, all the same. I'd have liked to pick up another and take it home, only I didn't want to seem greedy.

'I have a son too, you know. Like you – well, a bit bigger.'

'Where is he?'

The man nodded vaguely in the direction of the sea.

'Over there. Far away.'

'Does he write to you?'

'No. Never writes. Never has written.'

'Then how do you know where he is?'

'That's just it. I don't know. Never have known.'

He had an odd way of saying things. Repeating. 'Never has written – never have known.' A bit like poetry, sort of balanced. And like he'd said it all before, again and again. It made me feel sad. And yet, I didn't know what there was to be sad about. I had my stone, my little piece of the earth. Nothing to be sad about.

To comfort myself I bent down and picked up another stone. This one was long and slim, with all the corners beautifully rounded. It must have been in the sea a long,

long time; and yet I couldn't think how it had got up here, on top of the cliff. Perhaps one day there had been a huge wave, so great that it had washed right up over the cliff-top, carrying all these stones with it.

'Do you ever get any big waves, really big ones?'

'Oh, yes.' The man sighed. 'We get big waves all right.'

'Big enough to come right up to the cliff-top?'

'No, not that big. They don't need to be that big.'

'But they do! If they're going to carry the stones all the way up here.'

'Oh, that! That's not the question.'

'But it is,' I said. 'For, if it wasn't a wave, how did all these stones get up here?'

The man shrugged. He looked a bit puzzled.

'I don't know, really. I haven't the time to study all these things.'

This surprised me. Ever since we arrived days ago I'd seen the man standing there for hours at a stretch, just staring out to sea, doing nothing. How could he say he hadn't the time?

'What do you study, then?'

'The sea, the sea. I have to keep watching.'

'Watching for what?'

'You never know. There might be a storm coming. You never know. That's it, you see. You just can't trust it.'

He was silent again for a while, and I felt we'd lost each other. To fill in the time I began rubbing my two stones together. Then I started tapping the big one with the other.

The man must have heard, for he turned round and smiled at me. I was glad to see him smiling.

'Oh, so you've got another stone!'

'Yes. Is that all right?'

'Perfectly all right. We're not exactly short of stones in this part of the country.'

'We are at home. No stones to be seen.'

'You live in the town, then?'

'Yes. In a flat.'

'I see. So no stones. You can take as many as you like.'

'Thank you.'

He was looking at me thoughtfully, and he smiled again. It was a kind smile.

'Have you no one to play with?'

'No. I'm an only child. And my dad's not well enough to come out and play like he used to. That's why we've come to the seaside for our holiday. They say it might make him better.'

'I see. Well, remember to tell him you'll never go to sea. That'll help.'

That reminded me of his son.

'Has your son been away long?'

'A long, long time. Years.'

'How many years?'

'About twenty.'

'About twenty! That's centuries. It's more than twice my age!'

I thought about it for a little, while the man stared out to sea again.

'Will you recognize him, when he comes back?'

'Oh, yes. I'll recognize him all right. He won't have changed. But he may not recognize me. I'm an old man now. It makes a difference, you know. Twenty years.'

I wanted to say it must make a difference to his son as well. He too must be quite old by now – thirty, at least. But I thought the man might not like me to say that, so I kept quiet and began thinking about my stones again.

I was wondering how many I could take back with me. There would be enough room in my bag for quite a few. That would make it very heavy, but I'd carry it myself, so no one could complain. And at home I'd lay them all out on the window-sill, and that would be my own little bit of property. Real property, that is, a piece of the earth, not just things that belong to you, like your books and your clothes and your computer games.

Far away, I heard my name being called.

'It's my mum,' I said. 'I'd better go back.'

Before turning to run down to the cottage on the shore I added:

'Thanks for the stones. I'll come back tomorrow for more.'

But the man was gazing out to sea again and didn't answer.

Mum was standing at the garden gate, talking to the lady who lived in the cottage next door.

I showed them my stones and told them where I'd got them.

'And the man says I can have as many as I like.'

'What man?'

'The man standing up there on the cliff.'

'That'll be old Mr Curry,' said the lady. 'Always up there. His son was drowned at sea, and he's never got over it, poor soul.'

'But he's not drowned! Or, at least, the old man doesn't

know. He's still waiting for him to come back. And if the son is drowned, why don't they tell him?'

'Oh, they told him all right. More than twenty years ago.'

I went up to my little room looking out over the great, treacherous sea.

How could you know something and not know it?

I stood there a long time, while the tears trickled down my face and splashed onto what I now knew were the only two stones I would take away from this place, my dreams of property washed away by an enormous wave of alien grief.

50

The Goodness

You'll never make it to the top! Never! Even a young man could hardly do it. And you're in your eighties!

That's what they kept on telling me. And perhaps they're right. Perhaps I won't make it.

The old man stopped and looked down at a stone by the side of the road. Then he carefully placed the small bundle of clothes he was carrying beside it. He looked from one to the other, then opted for the stone and sat down on it.

For a moment a consideration of the relative virtues of the stone and the bundle of clothes took his mind off the alarming prospect before him.

Yes, I know, the stone's harder than the clothes. But that's what I like about it. There's a lot to be said for hardness.

Now, suppose this road were made of something soft, like sand, for instance, or mud, I wouldn't have a chance. Just look at it, winding all the way up the mountainside. Imagine my feet sinking in at every step, having to pull each foot out again – the effort, the unending effort.

No, there's nothing like hardness. You can depend on hardness. That's what sends your foot springing up again. It supports you, it keeps you steady.

Of course, it's like everything else, it's got its bad side too. Knives, for instance. They're sharp and strong and hard. They'd be no use without the hardness.

The old man sighed, and looked up at the track snaking its way up the mountainside.

If it weren't for those knives I wouldn't be here. I'd be sitting quietly at home, chatting to friends, looking after the hens, cooking a meal . . .

Pere had spend his whole life in the village at the foot of the mountain, cultivating his little plot. After his wife had died his son had tried to persuade him to come and live with him in the big city on the other side of the mountains. Pere had refused.

'You'll be lonely here, Father, with no-one else in the house.'

'I have my neighbours.'

'It's not the same as family.'

'I know, I know. But, what would a man like me do in a big city? Tell me that. All my life I've seen the sun rise over the plain ahead of me, and seen it set behind the mountain. And over there, where you live . . . It could never be the same, could it?'

His son smiled. 'No, Father. Over there it rises behind the mountains and sets over the sea.'

'There you are, then! I'd never get used to that, never. It would just feel wrong, wrong . . . I'd feel as if the sun was moving in the wrong direction. I'd feel something had gone amiss with the whole earth. Sort of upside down.'

So Manel had gone back to the big city, leaving his father sitting in the doorway, looking out over his tiny plot, with his hens busily scratching at the dry soil.

'This is my kingdom,' the old man had said just before they parted. 'There's nothing else I want out of life but just to sit here in peace and quiet.'

Just then a motor car had screamed round the corner beside Pere's house, as it turned sharply into the main road.

'Not all that peaceful these days, Father.'

'I know, I know. Things have changed.'

Now, sitting on his stone by the side of the road, Pere recalled that conversation. Perhaps I should have let him take me with him. Then I'd not be sitting here alone, with all these mountains to cross.

He looked down in the direction of his home. But by now he had come too far to see the village. Everything was unfamiliar already. And to think that he'd only just begun the journey!

A new life, that's what it is. At my age, a new life.

First would come this journey through the mountains. He'd been looking at them all his life, but never climbed so high. And then there would be the city to get used to. That seemed an even more terrifying prospect than the mountains.

But the knives were even worse.

Better get up and start walking again, or I won't make it to the next village before dark. All these kilometres between one village and the next! And I'm tired already!

Perhaps I shouldn't have been so stubborn. Perhaps I

should have yielded. Or perhaps I shouldn't have pan-
icked this morning.

He got to his feet, picked up his bundle, and set off
again, with a parting look at the stone he had been sitting on.

I'll never see it again, this stone I've been resting on.
Funny how much regret you can feel for something like
that, a mere stone by the roadside that you've rested on
for a while. It's become part of your life, part of your
memories. And it's only a stone! I'm leaving my whole
life behind me, and yet I feel as if I'd regret this stone
just as much as everything else.

The trouble was that he'd really not been able to take
in what was happening, it had all been so gradual – till
the last few, terrible days.

It was all the fault of the village for growing so much.
When he had got married he had built his own house, and
a very good one it was too, for their sort of folk, with
two rooms, just beside the village fountain. Only a few
yards back from the road, with their own little plot of
land round them. Most of the village houses at that time
had only one room, so they were very proud of their two,
he and his young wife.

That had been more than sixty years ago, and things had
changed. The village had prospered when they started
running a bus to the nearest town, and a lot of the men
got jobs there in the rope factory. They were quite well
paid, and spent a lot of their money on improving their
houses. In the end Pere's house, instead of being one
of the best, was the worst in the village. Pere had been
content to cultivate his own little plot instead of looking

for work in the town. So there had never been any money for improvements.

His wife hadn't minded, and after her death Pere cared even less. After all, it was nobody's business but his own.

That was what he thought, anyway. But when they built the new houses just behind his plot it was decided the best means of access would be by making a new road, cutting through not only his land, but his very house. That would get rid of the dangerously sharp corner that all the drivers were complaining about.

The mayor had come to see him.

'We'll rehouse you,' the mayor had said, looking important.

'But I don't want to be rehoused. I built this house myself, and I intend to die in it.'

The mayor turned nasty.

'You *will* die in it, if you don't get out before we knock it down.'

The argument became very heated. The mayor was the richest man in the village, with a reputation for ruthlessness. And he had set his mind on modernizing the village. A good approach to the new houses was essential.

His neighbours tried to persuade Pere either to accept the mayor's offer or to go and live in the city with his son. Pere refused both suggestions.

'The new houses are very nice,' they told him. 'They've all got a bathroom, even the smallest ones.'

'What do I want with a bathroom? I've lived without one all my life. No, I'm just not moving, not for anybody.'

And I thought I'd won. I knew they couldn't throw me

out. Not legally, at any rate.

And then the knives.

When he found the first one lying just inside his gate he thought someone had dropped it. A good machete, not the sort of thing one throws away. So he handed it in to the mayor's office, where people went to look for their lost property.

He got rather an odd look, but assumed it was just because of the dispute about the road.

Then, the following week, another knife. This time it was lying on his doorstep. That really shook him. He wasn't going to yield and move into one of the new houses, so he began to think about going to join his son. The trouble was, he had no money for the fare.

That night he wrote to Manel. He would post the letter in the morning and the money would arrive in a few days' time.

But that very morning he had found the third knife.

This one was sticking into the door.

There was no mistaking the symbolism. It was well known that the mayor was not above hiring a thug to eliminate opposition. There had been a few mysterious deaths no-one had dared look into too closely.

Pere had stood for a while gazing at the knife. Then panic had seized him. He'd made up a bundle of clothes, pocketed what little money he had in the house, and prepared some provisions for the road.

Then he went to say goodbye to his neighbours. They were horrified by his decision. Yes, all right, it would be dangerous to stay on in the house; but he simply had to swallow his pride and take the new house he was being offered. The journey over the mountains would be sheer madness.

'Perhaps that's what's wrong with me. Sheer madness. But I'm going all the same.'

The neighbours had kept on insisting that he must give in, go and see the mayor. They would help him move his things into the new house.

'No,' Pere insisted. 'I've already left my house – for good. My house and all that's in it.'

His feet were hurting, his back was beginning to ache. And he'd only been on the road for a few hours! He'd got several days' journey ahead of him, at the very least.

It's hard, having to give up all you've got. But then, life is hard.

Again he picked out a stone by the side of the road and sat down on it. And, after a moment's rest, his more meditative mood returned. He remembered his thoughts earlier on about the hardness of the stone.

Good and bad in the hardness, good and bad in the stone. And what about this other hardness that has forced me to leave my home and wander alone and helpless over these mountains? It's easy enough to see what's bad in that; but where's the goodness?

He was struggling to find the goodness; for Pere was a man who didn't like to think of himself as a victim. He had stood up to the mayor, and had intended to go on opposing him. But that third knife, stuck in the door, had plunged him into a state of sheer panic. For a moment he had felt the blade being thrust into him, the flesh parting, the blood spurting out. His hands had clutched at his heart, and when, a moment later, he had held them out and looked at them, he was almost surprised to see no blood.

And, as he looked at his trembling hands, he realized the decision had been made. He would leave his house, his village, his whole history. He would seek refuge with his son – dispossessed, a tramp.

So, where was the goodness? he now asked himself, sitting on a stone by the roadside, higher up the mountain than he had ever thought to be.

He noticed that the sun had passed its highest point, and got to his feet again.

Must keep going. I'll have to wait till later to find the goodness in what's happened. Perhaps I'll never find it. Perhaps some things are bad through and through. Things like having to leave your home in your old age and follow this lonely road over the mountains.

And it was indeed a lonely road. In the past it had been the only way from the village to the faraway city. But now they had a splendid new bridge over the river and a splendid new road leading to the city. So now this road was only used by the people who lived in the few tiny villages further up the mountain.

His neighbours had tried to persuade him to take the new road. He had refused, on the ground that it was much longer.

'But it's so busy,' they had said, 'someone would be bound to give you a lift.'

'Certainly not. I'm not a tramp!'

He had heard one of them mutter the word 'stubborn', and had ignored it. At the time this way had seemed the only way.

Now, walking wearily up the steep, rough road, trying

to justify his decision, it came to him that what he had needed most of all at the time was a gesture – a grand response to the enormity of the injustice meted out to him.

Yes . . . that's what it was, what it had to be. A way of answering the humiliation. That man was trying to prove I was nothing, a creature in his power. And, by taking the hardest way out of the situation, I've shown I have courage, and to spare; I've shown I have a mind of my own; I've shown he hasn't beaten me down.

For the following days, as he tramped mile after mile of the steep mountain road, sleeping in the primitive barn of some tiny village, on the floor of a shepherd's hut, and once in a cave in the mountainside, he thought little about anything except the sheer effort involved in keeping going.

It was only on the last lap, as he was trudging down the final mountain, with the big city lying at his feet, that he realized he was indeed going to make it.

For the first time he saw clearly that he had made the right choice, not only in deciding to leave the village, but also in choosing the mountain route. For life in the new house would have been intolerable, with the knowledge that everyone, himself above all, would know he had been forced to yield to an unjust power. He would have felt humiliated and diminished.

Better, much better, to have asserted his independence by walking out.

As for his choice of road . . . Well, he might have had a much easier journey, getting lifts from pitying strangers. But he would have been travelling as a beggar, humiliated. Whereas now, he realized from the astonishment and